The Christmas Quilt

Other Books in the Quilts of Love Series

THE CHRISTMAS QUILT

Quilts of Love Series

Vannetta Chapman

Abingdon fiction™
a novel approach to faith

The Christmas Quilt

Copyright © 2013 by Vannetta Chapman

ISBN-13: 978-1-4267-5277-3

Published by Abingdon Press, P.O. Box 801, Nashville, TN 37202
www.abingdonpress.com

Library of Congress Cataloging-in-Publication Data has been
requested.

Printed in the United States of America

1 2 3 4 5 6 7 8 9 10 / 18 17 16 15 14 13

To Martha Casbeer, my friend and a gifted quilter

Author's Note

While this novel is set against the real backdrop of Mifflin County, Pennsylvania, the characters are fictional. There is no intended resemblance between the characters in this book and any real members of that community. As with any work of fiction, I have taken license where needed in order to create the necessary conditions for my characters. My research was thorough; however, it is impossible to be completely accurate in details and description, since each community differs. Any inaccuracies in the Amish and Mennonite lifestyles portrayed in this book are completely due to fictional license.

Acknowledgments

This book is dedicated to Martha Casbeer. When I first moved to my town and asked around for someone who could help me learn to quilt, everyone gave me Martha's name. She has been invaluable to me in reading all of my manuscripts, but especially this one. Her patience is tremendous and her quilting skill a real treasure. Any mistakes in details regarding quilting are my own.

Melissa Neff and Sara Kalmbach provided insight into the nursing details.

I'd like to invite readers to visit www.locksoflove.org. This organization is mentioned in passing in this novel, and from what I have learned, it is a fine charity.

Thanks to my pre-readers: Donna, Dorsey, and Kristy. They do an excellent job of catching my mistakes. I also appreciate every member of my family and their patience with me when I'm working under a deadline. I'm indebted to my agent, Mary Sue Seymour, for always finding the best place for my work, and to the wonderful staff at Abingdon Press for publishing this story.

I enjoyed this return visit to Annie and Samuel and the fine folks in Mifflin County, whom you first read about in *A Simple Amish Christmas*. It's easy to grow attached to fictional characters when you spend so much time with them. My prayer is that these characters will bring you into a closer walk with our Lord.

And finally, may we give "thanks always for all things unto God and the Father in the name of our Lord Jesus Christ" (Ephesians 5:20).

Blessings,
Vannetta

But the fruit of the Spirit is love, joy, peace, patience, longsuffering, gentleness, goodness, faith, meekness, temperance: against such there is no law.
—Galatians 5:22-23

Prologue

Mid-October
Mifflin County, PA

Annie tried to quiet the nervousness in her stomach. She pressed her hand against the fabric of her new dress—her wedding dress. The fabric's bright blue color reminded her of the clear morning sky outside. From the upstairs window, she could see much of her parents' farm—the recently harvested fields, the barn, the yard, and the rows of benches where her family and *freinden* were waiting. The lane stretched past it all and led to the road that would take her to Samuel's, to her new life.

Soon she would be Annie Yoder.

A light tap at the door caused her to turn. Leah peeked inside. "Can I come in?"

"*Ya.* I was watching out the window, trying to freeze this moment in my mind."

Leah joined her there, linking their arms together. One year younger, slightly thinner, her hair a shade lighter, they could have been sisters. Annie's brother, Adam, had been courting her for over a year and already she felt like one of the family. Afraid her knees might give out, Annie sat on the bed.

"What's wrong?"

13

"You and I will be sisters soon, before the noon meal."

Leah reached forward and tucked a wayward curl into Annie's *kapp*. No matter how she pinned her hair, it insisted on escaping. Last night Samuel had confessed he'd loved her the moment she'd stepped into her father's room, when she'd come home to nurse Jacob, and he'd first seen her hair loose and cascading beneath her nurse's cap.

"You've known this for months," Leah reminded her.

"*Ya*, my mind knew, but today my stomach finally understands." She ran her hand over the hand-stitched quilt covering her bed, the bed she would no longer sleep in once she was Samuel's *fraa*.

"I'm nervous, too. The crackers I had for breakfast helped."

"I couldn't swallow a thing." Annie studied the blue and yellow pinwheel pattern of the quilt. "Do you think these feelings are normal?"

"It's the excitement. Think of all *Gotte* has in store for us. It seems Adam and I have waited for so long, and I know Samuel would have been content to marry you months ago—"

"I was so surprised when he asked me on Christmas."

"Today we begin our new lives."

Annie smiled as a calm assurance settled her nerves. "By this time next year we could have a family of our own."

"We're marrying on the same day." Leah stood and straightened her blue dress. "Perhaps we'll also share the day our babies are born."

1

Annie and Leah strolled along the sidewalk, peeking in the windows of the shops, enjoying the afternoon sunshine.

"When was the last time we had a day that didn't include freezing temperatures and snow dusting the doorstep?" Leah stopped suddenly as two young boys playing a game of tag ran around her.

"Maybe Saturday was the wrong day to come to town though. A weekday might have been better." Annie stepped closer and scowled after the boys. "Less traffic. Less *kinner*."

"It's not their fault I'm as big as Adam's workhorse."

"You are not."

"I am! Look at me . . ." Leah rested her hands on her stomach, which was quite large. She'd recently begun her seventh month of pregnancy, but a stranger might think she was in her final week.

"Belinda told you—"

"Twins take up more room. *Ya*, I know. But, Annie, I can't even put on my own shoes. Adam has to do it for me." Leah stuck out her bottom lip and lines formed across her forehead.

Annie knew that look—pure misery.

15

"I should have stayed home."

"You should have done no such thing. Let's go on to the general store, then stop by *mamm's* shop for some tea. Being out is *gut* for you and the babies."

"Says Nurse Annie—"

"Yes, she does."

"Who is four months pregnant and still not showing?"

The smile spread across Annie's face until she was giggling. Then they were both laughing, behaving like schoolgirls. Two pregnant women, standing in the middle of the sidewalk and causing traffic to stream around them.

"Four and a half months," Annie corrected Leah. "And she moved last night. Samuel and I both felt her."

"*She?* Of all people, you should know better than to predict whether your baby is a girl or boy."

"You're right, but Samuel seems so certain. After listening to him for four months, I've fallen into the habit of saying *she*." Annie hooked her arm through Leah's and pulled her along the sidewalk. "I need to purchase the lavender fabric for the nine-patch crib quilt I'm making you, and I happen to know Rachel received a shipment earlier this week."

"Oh, do we have to? I'm not sure what I need today is an encounter with Samuel's sister-in-law."

"I think she's mellowing." Annie whispered as they pushed their way into the general store, causing the small bell above the door to announce their arrival.

Instead of answering, Leah gave her *the look*. It was enough. After nearly three years back at home, back in Mifflin County, Annie had learned to read most of the unspoken cues from her sister-in-law. Packed with all of their previous conversations about Rachel, it said *you know she hasn't changed at all* and *we'll do our best to love her anyway* at the same time.

Annie didn't talk to many people about Rachel—her mother, Leah, and, of course, Samuel. No one had the answer, but they all knew prayer was the one thing capable of healing the wounded places in Rachel's heart. Until those places mended, chances were she would remain difficult and even occasionally somewhat nasty.

When they entered the store, a thousand memories surrounded Annie. Her family had shopped at the general store for as long as she could remember, but her recollection and what her eyes saw told two different stories.

The store she had visited as a child was crowded with delightful items in every available spot. Like most Plain folk, Annie had learned not to covet and to appreciate what she had rather than focus on what she didn't. Growing up, the general store had been owned by Efram Bontrager. She remembered it clearly—it didn't prick her desires as much as it sparked her imagination. When she walked over the doorstep, she'd always imagined herself stepping into an *Englisch* fairy tale. He carried supplies for Amish and *Englisch* alike, so all manner of things were on his shelves. Annie's favorite spot for years had been Efram's book nook in the front corner near the window. Her brother Adam had loved the old-fashioned candy counter with its jars of delicious penny candy.

Most of those items had vanished.

Two years ago Rachel Zook, Samuel's sister-in-law, had moved from Ohio—after her husband died. Annie knew from comments Samuel made it had not been a happy marriage. Rachel never talked about her life before moving—so Annie had no way of knowing if she was still mourning her husband or regretting that her two boys were being raised without the help of a father. There was a third possibility. Perhaps Rachel had fallen into a habit of discontent. She had simply shown up in Mifflin County one day. Efram had decided to put the general store up for sale so he could move closer to his family. Families in the community were hardly aware of Efram's plans, when Rachel bought the store and settled into the upstairs apartment with her boys.

The store had changed.

Rachel's store was clean and orderly and was stocked with items she was certain would appeal to the maximum number of customers. In other words, there were no surprises. The charm was gone.

Annie had to admit the place was cleaner.

"Leah, I'm surprised to see you out today." Rachel sniffed from her place behind the counter. Tall, thin, with a beautiful complexion only the scowl on her face could ruin, Rachel was dressed in her usual gray dress and black apron.

Why the sniff? Did she have a perpetual cold? Or was she suggesting they smelled bad? Annie knew they didn't, but she was tempted to check. Her mind went back to a psychology class she'd taken while pursuing her nursing certification, during the time she'd lived with her *aenti*, among the *Englisch*. The psychology instructor would have had a good time with some of Rachel's mannerisms.

"And Annie. I thought you were helping Belinda deliver the infant to the family on the south end of our district, though why Samuel would allow you to go scurrying around the county in your condition—"

"*Gudemariye*, Rachel." Annie aimed to keep her voice low and calm, as if she were speaking to a child. An image of Kiptyn immediately jumped to her mind, but she pushed it away. Although she'd had letters from her former patient for three years, she hadn't seen him since she'd left Philadelphia. She still missed the children she once worked with, and today wasn't a good time to focus on that loss. Today she needed to concentrate on making Leah's outing a pleasant one.

"I'd hardly call it morning." Rachel stared at the clock above the register, its hands ticking toward noon. She tapped the counter with her pen, as if to suggest they were late, or perhaps they were keeping her from something.

Annie glanced at Leah, who rolled her eyes. The immature gesture reminded Annie of her youngest sister, Reba. She nearly started giggling again, because Reba had not learned to abide Rachel's sternness. Reba insisted Rachel reminded her of the old bull out in the pasture—bad-tempered and mean.

The bell over the door rang out again. This time three young boys entered the store, but Rachel was having none of it. "Back out you go."

"But—"

"Not without your parents. Go and find them and then you may come back. I don't have time to keep my eye on you. I have work to do. Now out."

The boys—good boys who belonged to their church—tugged down on their hats and hurried back out the door. As they left, one murmured to the other two, "I told you she wouldn't let us come inside."

Annie plastered on her brightest smile. "I was hoping to pick up the lavender fabric for the quilt I'm working on for Leah's *boppli*."

"You haven't finished it yet?" Rachel tsk-tsked as she maneuvered behind the cutting table and pulled out the bolt of lavender cotton. It reminded Annie of the purple flowers which grew on the south side of her vegetable garden. "Are you sure you wouldn't rather use the off-white I carry?"

"*Nein*. This will be *gut*."

"I think I'll check and see what infant things you have. Maybe there's something I've forgotten." Leah waddled off down the aisle, her hand on top of her stomach as she went.

"You shouldn't have brought her to town." Rachel made no attempt to lower her voice as she unrolled the fabric with a thump, thump, thump that seemed to echo her disapproval.

"Do you honestly believe she'd be better off sitting at home? She has two months yet before the babies are due—"

"She won't make it two more months and both of us know it." Something resembling concern crossed Rachel's face, but when she glanced up at Annie, she blinked her eyes and whatever had been there, whatever she'd been feeling, had disappeared.

Possibly Annie had imagined it, or maybe for a moment Rachel had remembered what it was like to carry a child within her. Rachel's boys were older. Matthew had turned ten this year and Zeke was eight. The boys had adjusted to living in Mifflin County. They seemed to have adapted to life without a father—Rachel had moved to their town a year after her husband died. If there was a soft spot in Rachel's heart, it was for her boys, but she didn't show it often. Perhaps she was afraid of spoiling them. Where were Matthew and Zeke today? Samuel had reminded her to ask about them.

Certainly, a part of Rachel did remember the miracle of carrying a child inside for nine months and the hope life would turn out to be all you dreamed it could be.

"How much do you need?"

"Half a yard will be more than enough. I can use any extra on a patchwork quilt I plan to start after Christmas." Annie watched her measure and cut the fabric. "Probably you are right about Leah making it to term, but the *bopplin* will come when they're ready. It's *gut* for Leah to be out of the house and it helps her mood to—"

"Do not come in this store." Rachel paused in the middle of folding the fabric she had cut. For a moment, Annie wondered who she could be talking to—the bell over the door hadn't rung. In fact, the store was surprisingly empty for midday on a Saturday.

Annie angled her head to the right. When she did, she caught sight of her two nephews. The younger, Zeke, was halfway through the back door. Matthew stood behind him and had his hand on the door.

At the sound of their mother's voice, they both had frozen.

2

Leah had chosen a hanging bag for disposable diapers, decorated with farm animals and trimmed in lavender, blue, and green. She was walking back up the aisle when she heard Rachel's voice. It was a hard thing to miss, rather like the voice of a schoolteacher Leah had had in fifth grade. She'd been terrified of Sally Detweiler—a Mennonite woman who smelled like rubbing ointment and rarely smiled.

But she wasn't afraid of Rachel Zook.

Why were her two boys standing half-in and half-out of the back door?

They didn't seem frightened, exactly. Maybe disappointed.

"I know you are not done with your chores." Rachel didn't bother turning around, instead she directed her attention to the bolt of fabric she was finished with, a lovely lavender Annie would use on the crib quilt she was sewing. "Back outside until you're done."

"Yes, *mamm*." Both boys reversed direction, back toward the area behind the store.

Leah noticed that the older one, Matthew, was careful to catch the screen door so it wouldn't slam. What could their chores possibly be? What was there to do in the alley behind the store?

She rubbed her stomach, more to feel the connection with her *bopplin* than because they were causing her any discomfort at the moment.

What was it like for the boys to live in the apartment above the store? Did they miss having a yard to run and play in?

How did Rachel manage, raising them alone?

"I don't think you'll be needing the diaper holder, since you'll be using cloth. I've had Plain women try to use it for cloth diapers and they don't fit in it well, no matter how you fold them." Rachel moved to the register to ring up Annie's fabric purchase. "Though I do not enjoy discouraging you from purchasing something. I can use every sale I scrape together in this town."

Annie stopped at Leah's side as she studied the diaper holder. "Perfect colors. Matches the quilt I'm sewing."

"And the other your *mamm* is doing." Leah smiled and released the worries being around Rachel always brought to mind. "I still have some money left over from my vegetable booth."

"*Ya.* Your garden did much better than mine. I had that rabbit problem."

They started laughing again, but stopped when they realized Rachel was staring at them.

"Oh. I'm sorry. We're keeping you." Annie quickly counted out the amount showing on the register display. "Samuel wanted me to remind you about the luncheon at our house tomorrow."

"I couldn't possibly drive out—"

"*Onkel* Eli will be coming. He has to drive through town on his way to our place. He'll be happy to give you and the boys a ride."

Rachel's face scrunched up and she began shaking her head. "Oh, I don't know."

"My parents would so love a chance to see the boys. I believe *dat* has been working with Matthew on his checker skills."

Leah watched the interplay with interest. She understood all too well the stress that existed between Annie, who was now her sister-in-law, and Rachel, who was Samuel's sister-in-law. The fact that Rachel had tried to persuade Samuel to move to Ohio and marry her should have caused an insurmountable wall of jealousy between the two, but Annie had assured her it didn't.

Annie had said she and Samuel talked about everything—including the situation with Rachel.

It seemed to Leah that she hardly talked to Adam at all these days. He tumbled into bed exhausted, when he came to bed at all, and rose before daylight.

Glancing down at her stomach, which blocked the view of her feet, Leah couldn't help wondering if it was because of her size. She knew her husband loved her, but perhaps he didn't like her very much right now. Maybe things would be better between them in a few months.

"I suppose we could come if I didn't have to drive. I'd rather not use the mare and buggy more than necessary."

"*Wunderbaar*. It's settled then."

Leah made her purchase, without anymore commentary from Rachel, and was happy to see two more families enter the store as they were leaving. The last thing Annie needed was for Samuel to bear the financial responsibility of Rachel Zook and her two sons. The emotional baggage the woman had brought to town was enough of a burden.

Stepping outside into the November sunshine reminded Leah of being released from a long day at school. She stopped on the sidewalk, held her stomach in both her hands and pulled in a long, deep breath.

"*Was iss letz?*" Annie moved in front of her, reached forward and placed her palm against Leah's forehead. Then she moved her fingertips to Leah's wrist.

Leah knew Annie was counting her pulse.

Always the nurse, always checking on her.

Leah opened her eyes and smiled. "Rachel's store is a little oppressive."

"That's it?"

"*Ya.* Outside feels *gut.*"

"It does, but you scared me."

"You frighten easily, maybe because you are worried my babies will come early."

"Early, yes, but not today, Leah. Now let's go and have a cup of tea."

<hr />

Five minutes later, they sat down in the shop where Annie's mother worked. Leah had always been close to her own parents. Six months after she married Adam they made the decision to move to Wisconsin. She'd been completely shocked. It was something they had talked about for several years—because the cost of land was less there, but she hadn't thought they were serious.

Since then Leah's feelings toward Rebekah and Jacob had changed. Perhaps it was because her family had moved.

Maybe it was the fact that Annie was expecting her own first child, or because hers were twins.

Whatever the reason, in the last two years, she'd grown incredibly close to Annie and Adam's parents.

Rebekah moved toward them, calmness and joy on her face. "I was hoping you two would come in today. Let me help Charity see to the other tables, then I'll come and sit with you." Round, motherly, with gray hair peeking out from under her *kapp*, Rebekah Weaver was a balm to Leah's soul. They ordered and soon Rebekah was back, setting two mugs of tea in front of them and a plate filled with three kinds of cheese, crackers, and fruit.

"*Mamm*, we only ordered the tea—decaffeinated."

"No caffeine. I remember, and the lunch is on me. I have three *grandkinner* at this table. Can't start feeding them *gut* things too soon. I'll be back in a snap."

She was gone before they could argue.

"Your *mamm* is the best," Leah said, reaching for a cracker and some cheese.

"Our *mamm*."

"Right." Leah sighed, suddenly happy they had come into town.

"I love this cafe." Annie stared around the room as if she didn't come in to see her mother at least twice a month, as if she were seeing it with new eyes.

"What's not to love?"

"Did I ever tell you about the time Samuel followed me in here?"

"At least twice, but I don't mind hearing it again."

"I thought he'd gone crazy. I'd recently returned home, recently come back from Philadelphia. I hadn't even told my family yet about earning my nursing certification, and I was still all bound up with guilt. Samuel saw through all of those things. He saw something inside me I didn't even know existed." Annie set her package on the empty chair and reached for her tea. "Hard to believe we've both been married two years, Leah. Seems yesterday we were girls playing with our dolls on a summer afternoon."

Leah didn't answer; instead she studied the cracker she'd half eaten. Should she tell Annie about all the things worrying her? She didn't want to ruin their day out. And maybe it was nothing.

"Have you and Adam decided on names?"

"*Nein.*"

"Oh. Have you narrowed it down?"

Leah shook her head, certain if she spoke now, the tears would start.

Annie picked up the packages and moved them so she could sit in the chair beside her rather than across from her. "Leah, what's wrong? You were so happy a minute ago, out on the sidewalk, and now you look miserable."

"Maybe it's nothing . . ." Leah pulled the napkin out from under her silverware. Rebekah was finishing up with the last table of customers and she did not want to be blubbering when her mother-in-law joined them.

"Probably it is nothing, but I'm certain you'll feel better if you talk about whatever is weighing on your heart."

Leah nodded and rubbed at her eyes with the napkin. Rebekah headed toward them, and she didn't want to worry her. "Later. I'll tell you later."

"Promise?"

"*Ya.*"

"Everyone is served and it should be the end of what we call our lunchtime rush." Rebekah settled into the fourth chair with her own cup of hot tea. "Now show me what you purchased at the store."

Leah was relieved to focus on the baby things. Thinking of the babies eased the worries in her heart. Preparing for them helped her feel as if she were doing something useful.

Rebekah agreed that the diaper holder was perfect. "Folks think Amish don't use disposable diapers, but I'll tell you—with my five children it would have been a nice thing to have when we were going to church meeting or in town for shopping."

"Rachel didn't approve," Leah admitted.

"Oh. I wouldn't worry about what others think. It's not as if you're going to use them all the time. Cloth diapers are better overall, but there are situations when disposables will come in handy."

"If I have your blessing, that's *gut* enough for me. My *mamm* wouldn't give me an opinion when I wrote to her. I tried to describe the ones with the pull-tabs, but when she wrote back her comment on the subject was 'It wonders me' and nothing more! I couldn't tell if she approved or not."

"It's hard to understand some things from a letter, but I know your mother well, Leah. She isn't one to judge, so don't be worrying." Rebekah took a sip of her tea as she watched Charity to be sure she could handle the other three tables of customers. "Did you pick up your fabric, Annie?"

"*Ya*, let me show you." Annie pulled it from her bag, running her fingers over the soft cotton.

Leah could imagine what it would look like once she'd finished. She could see it lying in the cradle.

"What a pretty color. I've always favored purples," Rebekah said.

"It will be perfect for the nine-patch."

"You're using it for Sunbonnet Sue's dress, *ya*?"

"I thought I would. I haven't actually begun the quilt yet."

They all studied their food for a moment. Leah wasn't going to broach the subject that Rebekah was dancing around.

"Go ahead and say it, *mamm*."

"No, dear. I'm not about to say anything—"

"I know I'm running a little behind, but I'm a fast quilter once I begin . . ."

"I know you are. You've been busy, what with helping Belinda."

"And Samuel. You know I can't tell him no when he asks me to go along on his visits to care for someone."

Leah reached for a strawberry and popped it in her mouth. Her worries faded away as she listened to the good-natured bantering between Rebekah and Annie.

"Our community is so lucky to have the two of you." Rebekah straightened the tablecloth. "I knew when you came home from Philadelphia *Gotte* would use your talents in some special way."

When Annie stuffed the material back into the bag, Leah felt she should encourage her. "It's true, Annie. Your nursing comes in handy quite often. You were busy last week helping with the birthing of that calf over at David Hostetler's place."

"Birthing a calf. To think I went to nursing school—"

"Now, Annie. *Gotte* cares about the animals, too, and the vet couldn't be reached in time." Rebekah was trying to hide her smile behind her teacup. "Adam told me you enjoyed the birthing."

Leah's heart lurched. Adam had told her nothing of the calf's birthing. She'd heard about it from David when he'd stopped by to bring fresh milk, which he traded with them for eggs.

"I wouldn't say I enjoyed it. It was messy and frightening. I didn't exactly know what I was doing. Calves are bigger than babies and harder to birth in several ways. Fortunately, David and Samuel were there because another heifer was birthing at the same time. They needed an extra pair of hands."

"And yours were there," Rebekah added.

"They were." Annie grinned. "He was a white-faced calf, *mamm*. Pretty as shoofly pie."

"So, no quilting," Leah added.

"I mean to start this week." Annie pushed her plate away.

"You'll learn to set aside a specific time each day or evening for your sewing, which could be difficult since your schedule is never the same. Didn't you sit with Bishop Levi's mother one night this week?"

"We did. He brought her home from the hospital. There's nothing more they can do there, and it's *gut* for her to be at the farm where she at least remembers some things."

"How much longer does she have?"

"The doctors think a month or so, but Samuel says he's seen cases where the cancer can take one quickly or can cause them to linger. Samuel says there's no way to be sure."

"*Gotte* knows best."

"Why did you go, Annie?" Leah ran her finger around the rim of her cup. "If there's nothing to be done . . ."

"The bishop had to attend to a matter on the other side of our district and couldn't be back until the next morning, so we went and spent the night. It was no problem. Samuel and I took shifts. I like to go with him when I can. Once our *boppli* is born, I won't be able to share those times with him anymore."

"Everything changes when two become three." Rebekah smiled at them both. "Or four."

Leah's concerns always seemed out of proportion when she was visiting with Rebekah. Maybe she was right. Maybe at their home, things would change for the better.

"Once you cut your fabric, you can take it with you and quilt while you're waiting."

"*Ya.* I meant to, but then . . ." Annie stared down at her hands. "I took a nap instead. Three times last week. I know it's because of the *boppli*, but I feel guilty when I sleep in the middle of the day."

"Be glad you can, Annie." Leah rubbed her hands along her lower back. "It's been weeks since I have slept more than a few hours at a time in the evening, and not at all in the day."

"You girls will forget all about this as soon as you hold your newborn." Rebekah began stacking the dishes. "Annie, I'd be happy to help you begin the quilt."

"*Nein.* I want to do it myself. This is my gift. My work of love for Leah."

"All right." Rebekah nodded in agreement. "I understand."

Leah stood, with some difficulty, and collected her package from the store. "Let's go say hello to Charity before we leave."

"*Gut* idea."

"She can walk you girls back to your buggy." Rebekah pulled Annie, then Leah, into a hug.

When she did, Leah breathed in the smell of her freshly laundered *kapp*, cinnamon from the cooking she'd been doing in the back of the shop, and a dozen other things that all cried out *mother* to her. Something deep inside of her wanted to stand there, in Rebekah's arms, to rest and stop worrying.

"We'll see you tomorrow, at Annie's." Rebekah paused, reached out to touch her face, and then added, "If you need me before then, you send Adam."

Leah blinked and nodded. How could she have even thought of hiding anything from Rebekah Weaver? She had an instinctive way of understanding when anything was amiss among her children, and Leah was one of her children now. Though in the last months she had wondered about many things in her life—Rebekah's love was one thing she had never questioned.

3

Adam had completely disassembled the small gas-powered portable handsaw. You wouldn't think there could be so many pieces, but he had over twenty on the worktable in front of him. Nothing appeared broken, but there'd been enough dirt on the inside of the engine to keep it from working properly. He suspected when he put it back together, cleaned and oiled, it would run fine.

The sound of a horse and buggy pulled his attention away from the project.

Wiping his hands on his pants, he stepped out into the early afternoon sunshine.

"It's too nice a day for a farmer to be inside the barn," Samuel declared, unfolding himself from his buggy. At six feet tall and steadily gaining weight from Annie's cooking, he was a big man. The weight he needed to gain. For too many years, he'd resembled a scarecrow. For too many years—after the death of his wife and child in a winter storm, his grief had kept him from enjoying life.

"*Ya.* You're right it's a *gut* day to be outside, but my work is in the barn. Everything in the fields is done. You'd know since you helped me harvest."

Samuel slapped him on the back. "What engine are you taking apart today?"

"Small gasoline-powered handsaw."

"You don't say. Made by Ervin Hochstetler?"

"Who else?"

"Then we know it's a *gut* product."

"It is, but even a hand-saw made by Hochstetler has a limit to the amount of dirt it can handle. A mechanical engine is like the human body, Samuel. It has to be treated with respect—"

Samuel held up his hand. "No need to lecture me. I've heard you speak on this before, and I believe you."

Seeing what Adam had laid out on his workbench, he let out a long, low whistle. "Taking it apart I could probably do, but how do you put it back together?"

"It's not so hard. I always start at this end of the table." Adam indicated the right side of the bench. "Top to bottom, right to left. My process never varies. They go back together in the same order they came apart."

Together they walked the length of the bench until they came to the skeleton of the chainsaw.

"Not much left when you're done disassembling it."

"True. A few minutes before you arrived I'd finished cleaning all the parts. Now I'll go back through and put them together, being sure to properly grease each part as I do."

"You make it sound easy."

Adam ran his fingers through his beard. "I suppose a *gut* memory helps, but then you remember your herbs and what to give for which ailment."

"I have a few books I refer to," Samuel admitted, perching on a sawhorse.

"I have one or two myself. If I'm stumped, Leah and I will take a ride to the town's library."

"Leah's actually one of the reasons I stopped by. I wanted to see how she was doing."

"Oh." Adam glanced toward the house, shook his head, and then focused on the engine again. "She and Annie aren't back from town yet."

"Didn't figure they would be. I saw Belinda yesterday and she updated me on Leah's medical stats." Samuel ran his palm over the sawhorse. "Belinda was the one who suggested I stop by and talk to you."

"To me?" Adam's voice squeaked like the hinge on the back kitchen door Samuel had been intending to oil. "Why talk to me? I know next to nothing about pregnant women."

Samuel laughed. "Pregnant women, maybe, but I imagine you know plenty about Leah."

"You might be surprised." Adam began piecing the small engine back together. Working on the engine felt good. At least it was one thing he was confident he knew how to do. "Why would Belinda send you to talk to me?"

Though the day was cool, suddenly sweat beaded along Adam's forehead. "Is something wrong? Is that why you're here?"

"Nothing's wrong. Belinda thought maybe Leah wasn't being completely open with her. Maybe she wasn't feeling well or she was worried about something. Belinda tried to get her to talk, but Leah clammed up tighter than a silo in a winter storm. So she asked me to come and talk with you—see if there's anything she should be concerned about. We want this pregnancy to go as smoothly as possible. No surprises."

Adam stopped pretending he could focus on the engine. At this rate, he'd make such a mess of things it would likely resemble an *Englisch* blender when he was done with it. Sticking his hands in his pockets, he turned and trudged toward the open door of the barn. The sunshine on his face helped. It didn't provide any of the answers he'd been searching for, but it helped.

"Adam? Are there any surprises we should know about? It's difficult enough to birth twins at home. If there's anything you can tell us—"

"Surprises? Seems to me there's been nothing but surprises since the day Leah learned she was carrying my child." The words weren't easy for Adam to speak. They echoed in the barn, sounding to him like a confession, but he wasn't sure exactly what he was guilty of. If he had known, he would have gone to the bishop already. As it was, he continued to toss sleeplessly each night—usually on the couch in their small living room.

Samuel joined him in the patch of sunlight coming through the doorway of the barn. "She was sick at first. I remember that."

"You make it sound as if she had a cold. It was so much worse, Samuel. Leah spent several hours each morning in the bathroom, clutching the toilet. I'm grateful we don't live in a district that still insists on outhouses or my wife would have caught pneumonia, she spent so much time in there."

"I'm sure it must have been hard—"

"I wasn't allowed in there," Adam continued. "For two years, nearly three, we shared everything. Suddenly, she didn't want me near her. As if she was embarrassed."

"Maybe she was."

Adam reversed direction, nearly bumping into Samuel. "Why would she be embarrassed? It wasn't her fault the babies were making her sick. We didn't even know at that point there were two . . . two, Samuel. Do you realize how exciting it is, and how terrifying? I'm not sure I can be a *gut dat* to one, but we'll have two at the same time."

"Let me see if I have this straight." Samuel walked out into the sunshine, to the pasture fence where he could see the workhorses Adam had allowed out for the afternoon. "Leah had a bad case of morning sickness, which lasted longer than most. It had barely ended when you learned she was pregnant with twins."

"*Ya*, I suppose the timing is about right."

"How have things been since then?"

Adam noticed that Samuel wasn't limiting his questions to asking about Leah anymore, but he didn't call him on it. "I don't know. How are things supposed to be with a pregnant woman? She doesn't sleep well, so most nights I sleep on the couch. I don't want to wake her when I get up at the crack of dawn."

"And her moods?"

Adam threw his hands up in the air. "About the same as a donkey you might be tempted to purchase. Not that I'm comparing my *fraa* to a donkey, though her temperament is similar."

Samuel grinned. "Cranky is normal."

"Oh, not always cranky. Sometimes she cries on top of the temper."

Samuel laughed outright. "You're giving me something to look forward to with your *schweschder*. You know that, right?"

"You're the doc for our district—"

"I'm not a doctor, Adam."

"Fine—herbalist. Whatever you want to call yourself, you've helped Belinda birth plenty of babies—you've birthed them yourself when she couldn't be there. I'd think you would be used to pregnant women."

Samuel pushed his hat more firmly on his head as a buggy pulled into Adam's lane. "Tending to a woman who is expecting a child is one thing. Living with her is another completely."

"That's it? That's the best advice you can give me?"

They moved together toward the women. "I'm not going to pretend I have the answers, Adam. Leah needs to know you love her. The *bopplin* will be born soon and you'll have more sleepless nights ahead. Before you know it though—you'll have your bride back."

Adam wasn't so sure about that, but when Leah first caught sight of him, when she raised her hand and waved and the smile he knew so well covered her face—he temporarily forgot about all the things that usually stole his sleep. For that moment, he could trust what Samuel had just told him was true.

Annie was anxious to get home and speak with Samuel. Leah had finally opened up to her a little on the ride home from town. She didn't think her *bruder's* wife had shared everything bothering her, but she'd shared enough. She'd liked to have stayed and fetched a rolling pin and threatened Adam with it.

Somehow, she didn't think that was in keeping with the *Ordnung*. Too bad, because Adam was one stubborn guy—she should know from her years growing up in the same house with him. Maybe Samuel would have some ideas on how to talk some sense into him. Maybe Samuel had experienced similar feelings when his first wife, Mary, was pregnant.

Annie didn't bring up Mary and Hannah often. She didn't want to break open old wounds, and it would seem the death of his wife and child, though the accident had been over ten years ago, would still be a painful thing. Samuel had made it clear when they married that no topic was off-limits. She trusted him when he said it; however, she would only ask about Mary if it seemed prudent to do so. Perhaps Samuel would have some ideas about her *bruder* without having to broach how he had reacted to his first wife's pregnancy.

So far, he'd been perfectly patient with her.

But then, she'd had none of the complications Leah had endured.

Yet.

Thankfully, they had nothing scheduled for the afternoon except a simple meal for dinner. They had done the cleaning for tomorrow's luncheon the day before. She might also have time to work on the quilt. She was happy with her pattern. If she could gather the correct templates, maybe she could begin on her sample square.

Pulling into the lane to their home, Samuel's buggy tagging along behind hers, she was surprised to see a buggy waiting near their front porch.

She didn't recognize the buggy at first, but as she drew closer, she did recognize the couple—

Jesse and Mattie Lapp. They lived on the outer edge of their district. An older couple, in their sixties, they seldom came to town for anything other than the twice-monthly church meeting.

Annie didn't bother driving her buggy to the barn. She pulled up beside them, barely taking time to wind Beni's reins around the front porch railing. Fortunately, her mare was well trained and content to be home.

The Lapp's mare, however, seemed agitated. Annie took a moment to pat the neck of the animal and murmur a word of peace to her. Mr. Lapp was still in the front seat of the buggy, though it was plain he had not been driving. Mattie had been. Now she was hovering over her husband, whispering to him. She didn't so much as glance up as Annie approached their buggy.

"Jesse. Mattie. Is everything all right?"

Samuel was beside her by the time she'd reached the door and peeked inside. Annie could tell immediately that something was terribly wrong. Jesse lay back against the buggy seat. His breathing was shallow and his skin clammy and pale.

"I'll fetch my bag," Samuel whispered. "Don't attempt to move him."

"How long have you been here, Mattie?"

"Maybe thirty minutes. We didn't know where else to go. Jesse was having the pains again, so we waited for them to pass. When they didn't . . ." Her hands came out and fluttered around as if she had no control over them. Though she was talking to Annie, her eyes never left her husband's face. She seemed afraid to glance away, afraid to take her eyes off him even for a second. "I didn't know what to do. He didn't want to get in the buggy, but I didn't know what to do. I made him get in. Practically had to drag him. Was that the right thing to do, Annie? He won't talk."

"You're talking enough for both of us, woman."

Mattie was Annie's height and still worked hard around her farm each day. She had added weight through the years, but her arms were strong. Annie had no trouble picturing her hitching up the wagon and driving it to their porch steps, before dragging Jesse up into it. How long would that have taken?

Annie allowed a small smile. "It seems he hears us fine."

She angled around Mattie. "Jesse, I want you to lie down across the buggy seat. Can you do that for me?"

The fact that he didn't argue with her was a worry. What Amish man would lie down in the front of his buggy without protesting? If she had been compiling a chart, she would have written that Jesse's appearance was similar to most men in their sixties who had the potential for heart problems. Though thin men certainly had heart problems, it seemed to Annie that often there was a particular shape, whether *Englisch* or plain. Jesse had it—the pear-shaped stomach and barrel chest. It was a stereotype, but as one professor had taught her, "medical stereotypes exist because they are often true."

Mattie's hands fluttered over his chest, his beard, his cheeks. "Ohhh. Ohhh, he's dying isn't he? I know it. Oh, my sweet Jesus. He's headed home."

"Mattie." Annie automatically fell into the role of nursing. She kept her voice calm but firm. "Mattie, look at me."

Samuel was back. Annie had to pull Mattie out of the buggy so Samuel could squeeze in and use his stethoscope to check Jesse's heart rate.

"He's dying, Annie." Mattie's voice rose to a near wail. "He promised never to leave me, and he's dying."

"Mattie, I need you to help us. Can you do that?"

The older woman swiped at the tears flowing down her face, pushed her hair back into her *kapp,* and nodded.

"I need you to go into the house and wet a cloth. Wet two. Wring them out well so they're not dripping and bring them back. Also, bring me a glass of water. Samuel will have some aspirin for Jesse to take and he might like a sip of water."

Mattie nodded but remained frozen in place.

"We'll stay with him, Mattie."

"What if he goes? What if he goes while I'm gone?"

"We're with him, honey. You go for the cloth. And don't forget the glass of water."

As soon as Mattie was hurrying toward the house, Annie pushed her head back into the buggy. Samuel was crouched in the floor area and Jesse was still lying across the seat. "Heart attack?"

"Appears to be. Jesse, how are you feeling?"

"Not so *gut*." He didn't open his eyes, but his voice had gained some strength.

"Blood pressure's too low," Samuel muttered. "Jesse, have you been prescribed any nitroglycerin pills?"

Jesse shook his head no.

Annie heard the front screen door to their house slam shut. She glanced up in time to see Mattie running toward them, running with the cloth and glass of water.

Samuel pulled the bottle of baby aspirin from his medical bag. "I want you to chew two of these for me. They're going to help."

Jesse struggled to sit up. Annie hurried around the buggy in order to position herself behind him. As she rushed around the back of the buggy, something told her she might be too late. When she arrived at the other side and saw the expression on Samuel's face, she understood then what had started as a beautiful winter Saturday was turning into one of tragedy.

4

Annie stared at Samuel as Jesse clutched his chest.

Mattie hadn't quite reached the buggy, but she would in another few seconds. She would see Jesse was having another heart attack.

"Annie, run to the barn. Use the phone to call 9-1-1. Go now!" Samuel's voice was calm, but it received no argument. He'd dropped the unopened bottle of aspirin back into his bag and had already begun loosening Jesse's collar. When Jesse slumped back against the seat, slumped back lifeless, Samuel began to administer CPR.

Annie backed out of the buggy, nearly tripping over her dress.

Mattie saw her and stopped. She dropped the glass of water and the dish towel in the dirt. "Where are you going?"

"To the barn. Help Samuel!" Annie ran, thanking *Gotte* as she did that the bishop had allowed the phone installation a year ago. It was a phone much like those in the shacks dotting the countryside throughout the community. Bishop Levi had decided that with Annie and Samuel married, and with them both helping meet the medical needs of their district, it was prudent to allow the exception to their rule of no phones.

She ran and placed the call even as she heard Mattie's crying. And as she went through those motions, she prayed—for *Gotte's* help. For Samuel's strength, so he could continue performing CPR until the ambulance arrived. For Mattie, so she would feel a sense of calm. For Jesse, so his heart would beat again. For herself, so she would know how to help.

For *Gotte's wille*.

The emergency dispatcher informed her it would take ten to twelve minutes for an ambulance to reach their address.

She hung up the phone and returned to Samuel, but this time she didn't run. This time she was more mindful of the child she was carrying inside her, though she didn't think running would hurt her. Many pregnant women were joggers, but she wasn't used to running—and this was a stressful and emotional situation. So, instead of running, she walked quickly and focused on remembering all of her training on the cardiac ward.

It had been a mere six weeks' rotation.

And it had taken place over three years ago.

In the hospital, they had an external defibrillator, which she had used one time. She and Samuel weren't equipped with any such device. There would be no way to administer an electrical shock to Jesse's heart if it had stopped beating completely. No, they could only do their best to provide what medical care they were able and continue the CPR, which she could see Samuel was still performing.

"I can do that," she whispered. "They trained me at Mercy Hospital."

"*Nein.* I'm *gut.*" Sweat was beading on his brow. How long had he been at it? Three minutes? Four?

Mattie sat on the ground beside the buggy, weeping and praying. The German words flowed out of her, out from her heart and onto the cold ground.

Annie crawled into the buggy, placed her fingers gently against Jesse's wrist though she didn't expect to find anything. "Samuel! He has a pulse. It's weak, but—"

Samuel stopped pumping on Jesse's chest and placed his stethoscope there. "*Ya*. His heart is beating. How long until the ambulance arrives?"

"Five, maybe six, minutes."

"Try to get a blood pressure for me."

She was already slipping the cuff over his arm.

Jesse began to stir, though he didn't speak.

"Glad to have you back, Jesse." Samuel knelt beside him in the buggy, next to Annie in the floor area, which was no easy task. "You gave us a quite a scare."

Jesse said nothing, but he did chew the aspirin Samuel slipped into his mouth. Mattie popped up at Jesse's name.

"Is he alive?"

"He is, Mattie. It would seem that *Gotte* heard your prayers."

Pressing the top of her head to the top of her husband's, she began weeping in earnest.

Annie raised her eyes from Jesse, from monitoring him, to glance at Samuel. They shared one of those priceless moments, a heartbeat of life she understood was precious. It would stand out in her memory even when she was old and the curls beneath her prayer *kapp* were gray. It reminded her of the time they had helped to birth Faith and Aaron's baby—the first miracle they had witnessed together. Surely, this was another.

At that moment, the ambulance hurried down the lane, lights flashing and siren blaring.

"You update them." Samuel nodded. "I'll stay here."

She ducked out of the buggy and met the paramedics as they were pulling their equipment from the rig. Two young men in their twenties, they didn't seem surprised to be treating a heart attack victim in a buggy or being updated by an Amish nurse. Annie imagined they had seen it all.

Within fifteen minutes they had Jesse stabilized and Mattie in the back of the ambulance beside him, holding his hand. An intravenous drip had already improved his color.

"What about our horse and buggy?" Mattie said, as the paramedics prepared to close the doors to the ambulance.

"We'll take care of both," Samuel assured her. "And we'll send word to your place for someone to tend to the other animals. You stay with Jesse. They'll most likely need to do surgery."

As a look of anxiousness washed over Mattie's face, Samuel stuck his head farther inside. "Keep praying and so will we. I imagine the bishop will arrive at the hospital before the surgery. You're not alone in this, Mattie."

He helped shut the door on the back of the ambulance, and then it pulled away and left behind a river of silence.

They stood there, a few feet apart, watching it go.

Samuel turned and studied her until Annie grew self-conscious—suddenly aware of the dirt on her apron, the way her curls had escaped her *kapp*, and how sweaty she had become, even in the cold.

Finally, he closed the gap between them and laced her fingers in his, before leading her up the porch steps.

"You did very well, Nurse Annie."

The blush started slowly, until it crept all the way up her neck and along her cheekbones. When had Samuel last teased her by calling her *Nurse Annie*?

"Thank you, Doctor."

"You were quite professional during that crisis."

"As were you."

"For a moment there I thought we were going to have two heart attacks on our hands—both Jesse and Mattie." He led her inside and insisted she sit at the table as he poured them both a glass of water.

"Can you imagine it though, Samuel?"

He didn't answer, only waited and watched her.

She pushed on. "It was as if her heart was breaking as his was stopping. It was as if they were one."

Annie sipped the water. "I suppose such a long marriage creates a strong bond. *Ya?*"

Samuel finished his water and set the glass in the sink. Instead of sitting beside her, he squatted in front of her chair, pulled her hand forward, and kissed her palm. "I think each year that passes, two hearts become more entwined, like two vines growing side by side. Eventually it must become difficult to know where the beat of one stops and the beat of the other begins."

Tears blurring her eyes, Annie nodded.

Samuel reached forward and kissed her on the forehead.

"Now I have three buggies to see to," he said, standing and grinning. "If I'm not mistaken I saw some quilting items in your bag."

"For Leah's *bopplin*."

"I'll fetch it for you. Unless you'd rather nap?"

"*Nein*. I think I'd like to sew. I prepared dinner before we left. I'll place it in the oven, then go upstairs and work on her quilt."

"*Wunderbaar*. How long does the food need to cook?"

"It's chicken. I'll set it for about two hours." Annie went to the gas-powered refrigerator and began foraging around in it, but as Samuel crossed the kitchen to head out the front door, she had to call out to him.

It wasn't their way to speak of feelings openly. It was enough to work beside each other every day. But after this, after so close a brush with death, she felt a strong need to express what was pushing up against her heart, against her baby.

He stopped, his hand on the door, an expression of surprise on his face.

Her eyes met his as she cradled the chicken casserole in her arms. "I love you, Samuel."

"And I love you, Annie."

———— ⌘ ————

Thirty minutes later, she was upstairs sitting in what she thought of as her sewing room. The top floor of her and Samuel's house had the staircase coming up through the middle section, surrounded by three bedrooms and a bath. He'd purchased it years ago from an Amish farmer who had a growing family—there were four bedrooms, including the one downstairs. There were also two bathrooms—one upstairs, one downstairs. Annie realized many Amish still used outhouses. Leah's family had recently moved to Wisconsin and some of the communities there didn't allow indoor bathrooms. She'd always had indoor facilities and thought it would be a big adjustment to use the outdoor ones—though, of course, theirs was nothing like the *Englisch*. The water came out slowly when you turned it on and sometimes there wasn't as much hot water as she would have liked, but it was still better than an outhouse!

Their bedroom faced the north, with windows peering out over the yard and the lane. Annie loved the view. She adored waking up each morning and imagining what might be in store, what might be coming down the lane. The bedroom next to theirs, the one with the windows facing east, she had decided to make into their nursery. Although she planned to keep her infant in a cradle in their room for the first month, she didn't intend to keep her there for long.

It didn't take *Englisch* training to convince her of the need for babies to be in their own bedrooms. Her mother had been quite free with advice! "Parents need privacy, Annie. You keep your infant close until her feedings are down to once a night, then put her in her own room at night. You'll hear her if she cries, and you and Samuel will still have your time for intimacy."

Annie smiled at the memory as she laid out her material for Leah's quilt. The third bedroom, the one across from theirs and with a small window facing south, had seemed perfect for a sewing room. She'd argued they might need it for another baby, but Samuel had said, "One year at a time, Annie."

So he and Adam had carried the heavy treadle machine up the stairs, and he'd made her a fine table for laying out her patterns and cloth.

The pattern. She'd set her heart on a nine-patch crib quilt. Her mother had made an all-hearts naive crib quilt for the other twin. That pattern called for three squares across, four rows down, and hearts appliquéd in every other square. Annie had seen it last week, and she wanted to complement the traditional Amish colors her mother had used.

In fact, remembering the pattern her mother had chosen, and studying the pattern in front of her, she thought it might be nice to put a heart somewhere in the quilt she was making and she did happen to have a template for a heart appliqué.

Her nine-patch pattern called for her to alternate a Sunbonnet Sue and Overall Sam in each square. Perhaps she could adjust her pattern so that she could place a heart in one of the squares, then it would coordinate with what her mother had sewn. After all, she was following a pattern, but more than that, she was making something special for her niece, or maybe her nephew.

She smiled at the thought.

And her mind darted back to Jesse Lapp.

How was he? Was he even now on the surgery table?

Was Mattie alone in the waiting room or had Bishop Levi made it there to stay with her—to pray with her, strengthen her and be a comfort?

Annie propped her chin in her hand and gazed out the window, toward their barn. The door was open. Samuel had moved both of their buggies inside, but the Lapp's mare was giving him some trouble. Samuel stood there, between the house and the barn. He appeared to be talking to the animal, holding a bucket of oats in one hand and brushing her mane with the other hand.

Life was like that, wasn't it? Sometimes easy. Other times difficult. The unexpected happened, and then you did your best to help each other through it.

She was worried about Mattie, and she was also concerned about Leah and her babies. Maybe she could pray while she quilted, pray, and put her concerns aside as she decided which colors to place on which pieces of the quilt. Adding the heart appliqué was a good idea. It would help to convey to Adam and Leah how much these children were going to be loved.

The ray of sun through the window had slid down the wall, and Annie realized her time for sewing was coming to a close for the day. She needed a few more minutes to finish planning her quilt—choosing which colors she would use for which pieces of the pattern on Leah's quilt. She had enough light to find what she needed.

She searched through her basket of fabric again. Where was the dark blue? She had some left over from the quilt she'd sewn for the charity auction last summer—at least a yard, which would be enough if she cut her pattern carefully. Maybe it had fallen behind the sewing table Samuel had constructed for her.

Setting aside the basket, she lowered herself to the floor carefully. She wasn't yet in the fifth month of her pregnancy, barely even showing, but she'd promised her husband and her *mamm* she'd stop hopping around like a jackrabbit. As a nurse, she knew exercise was good for her baby. It was easier to appease her *mamm* than argue though. Once on the floor, she proceeded to crawl around on her hands and knees, searching under the table for the fabric.

"Lose something?"

"Samuel!" Annie popped up, knocking her *kapp* nearly off her head and releasing a cascade of curls.

"Let me help. What are you searching for down there?" Samuel's tone was scolding. After nearly two years of marriage Annie recognized it, but his eyes were laughing with her.

"Fabric. I seem to have lost some, but . . ." Spying a splash of blue in the back corner, she snatched at it and stood up. "Found it."

"I could pull the table away from the windows. Then you'd be able to see behind your treadle machine."

"*Nein.* I love the view and the light is *gut* here."

"Usually *gut*, when there aren't so many shadows."

They both looked out the upstairs window of the farmhouse. A giant maple tree blazed with red, gold, and brown leaves winked in the last of the winter sunlight.

"*Ya*, the afternoon slipped away from me," she agreed. "But I'd rather the machine stay where it is."

"All right, but next time let me hunt for any lost fabric."

"Agreed."

Samuel studied the pieces she'd laid out—lavender, purple, two greens, two blues, black, and white. "Let me think. The colors suggest a manly sort of quilt."

"Manly? Did you see the purple?"

"You're adding that dark blue."

"You know it's the baby quilt for one of Leah's babies. I told you I was working on it before you went to the barn."

"What type of pattern?" Samuel asked, combing his fingers through his beard.

"A nine-patch crib quilt. I wish I had started earlier."

"So I shouldn't expect it for my Christmas gift?"

"No, you shouldn't." Annie's cheeks reddened in spite of herself. Samuel's gift was finished and hidden already—a slate gray sweater she'd spent all of October knitting.

"Leah's babies are due—"

"December 28th," Annie finished for him. "We talked about my tardiness today and she laughed. Everyone says I'm a fast quilter."

"Twins often make an early appearance, it's true, but I wouldn't worry too much. It's only a quilt, *mi lieb*."

"I know. I'd like to have it finished before they're born though." Annie began stacking the fabric carefully.

"And I know you'll do your best." Samuel peered at her pattern as if it were a book on herbs, but she knew he was thinking of something else. "No worries, Nurse Annie. Soon enough your project will be done and our midwife will call for your help delivering your niece and nephew."

"How do you know they will be a girl and a boy?"

"She's carrying them low. I've seen it before." Samuel winked as he shifted closer to her, lacing his fingers with hers. "Once you start on something you tend to focus on it wholeheartedly. I suspect you will finish your quilt for the *bopplin* early."

"I do have plenty of time, at least six weeks. I was there when Leah went for her prenatal visit last week."

"And everything's *gut*? Because I spoke with Belinda earlier today and she seemed to think—"

"The doctor told Leah there's nothing to worry about. I'm glad she agreed to see the doctor, even though she plans on using Belinda to deliver the *bopplin*." Annie started to tell him about her and Leah's conversation in the buggy. Was this the right time though? It wasn't actually about Leah's physical condition.

"*Wunderbaar.*" Samuel patted his stomach. "Would you like me to help you with dinner?"

"Dinner! Samuel, I forgot about the casserole." Annie attempted to pull her hand from his, to hurry past him and out of the room, but he caught her in his arms.

"No need to rush. I checked it when I came inside. Smelled burned, so I took a peek."

"Burned?" Her voice rose like a screech owl.

"Appeared mostly black. I think you'll have to leave it all for me."

Annie ran her palm along his cheek, then leaned forward and kissed him once. "It wasn't burned," she whispered. "I would have smelled it."

"Maybe not black," he admitted.

She kissed him again.

"I confess. The chicken was brown and the potatoes seasoned perfectly. Would you like me to go down and finish things up?"

"I would not." She slapped him on the arm and pushed past him. "I can prepare dinner for two."

"Three soon enough," he called after her.

"Yes, three." She smiled to herself as she heard him running water in the bathroom sink. They would eat, then spend a quiet evening together.

She would tell him her worries about all Leah had said after they ate. Samuel would know what they should do, if anything. Quilting for the afternoon had been exactly what she needed to spend a few hours doing. Though she hadn't started sewing yet, focusing on the fabric and the pattern had helped calm her nerves.

Now to feed her starving husband.

5

Sunday morning should have been relaxing. Since this was not their Sunday for church meeting, Leah didn't have to hurry, which was a good thing. The babies felt as if they were fighting for space inside her stomach. Belinda had warned her these last few weeks would be even more uncomfortable. Leah hadn't thought that would be possible. As she lay in bed, staring around her belly at her ankles, she decided they were definitely less swollen than the day before.

Maybe today would be better.

Maybe the worst was behind her.

And maybe she and Adam wouldn't argue again.

Struggling out of the bed, she tried to picture the babies—healthy and sleeping in their crib.

With her hand, she caressed the mound that was her stomach. "You're worth every minute of discomfort," she whispered.

By eleven o'clock that morning she wasn't so sure. Her body was rebelling against her. It felt like a buggy she couldn't quite control as she tried to make her way around the house.

Soon she found herself seated beside Adam on the way to Annie's—beside him but not next to him. He'd placed the casserole bowl on the seat between them. Had he done that on purpose? Less than a year ago he'd always insisted she sit right beside him, tucked up close.

Not anymore.

She stared down at her feet—or in the direction of her feet. Her ankles had begun swelling as soon as she'd started making breakfast, which he'd eaten standing at the kitchen counter. Adam had tried to help her put on her shoes, but they'd had no luck. That was when the first tears had started and when he'd first become frustrated with her. Who could blame him? She weighed nearly as much as the heifer in the barn, and she acted like a calf—bawling at the smallest thing.

"Think anyone will notice I'm wearing shoes with no laces?" she asked. They were halfway to Annie's. She had wanted to stay home, but he'd insisted that she come to the family luncheon. Maybe, just maybe, he did want to spend the day with her.

"My family?" Adam snorted. "If there's food on the table, chances are they won't notice what's underneath it."

"Unless one of Reba's animals gets loose."

Adam smiled and some of the tension in Leah's heart loosened. "It's been a while since that happened. Once she started helping at the veterinary office in town, I believe she stopped placing critters in her apron pockets."

Leah stared out over the fields they were passing. The weather had turned colder and it looked to her as if snow might be threatening. She was ready. Snow meant Thanksgiving and then Christmas. Soon after Christmas would be the arrival of their children.

"I should have made something else to bring. My bowl of pudding hardly seems enough considering all the people who will be there."

"You worry too much." The words came out sharply. "No one expects you to cook at all with the *bopplin* nearing their due date."

Cooking was the one thing she could still do! Leah thought of mentioning that to Adam. She almost brought up the fact that long hours doing nothing but knitting weren't necessarily a blessing, but she bit the words back. The last thing she wanted was to argue this morning. This was Sunday, and though Adam's time in the barn had cut short their Bible study, she wanted the rest of the day to go perfectly.

Some days she found herself so bored she thought she might go crazy. She realized complaining about too little work was *narrisch*. In the old days—before she was pregnant, she'd go to the barn and help Adam. The last time she'd tried that, he'd shooed her away, telling her she might get hurt out there.

Leah cleared her throat. "I meant to say I should have prepared something more last night, since I had the time. If I had known you weren't going to make it in to eat dinner, maybe I could have focused on baking a cake or—"

"Do not start on me again about last night."

"Adam, I wasn't."

"I cannot help it if sometimes things don't go as planned, Leah. The engines, they don't always work once I put them back together, and you know we are barely making it with the money from the crops."

Leah stared at him, stared at this man it seemed she didn't even know anymore. Where was her Adam with his easy smile and carefree spirit? The Adam who had taken her for a picnic on the foundation of their home before the walls were even finished. Tears spilled down her cheeks, and though she knew she should let it go, she couldn't help asking the question that had kept her tossing and turning until the wee hours of the morning.

The same question they had argued about last night.

The question he had yet to answer.

"And is that why you had to leave so late in the evening, Adam? Because of your engines?"

"Leah, I will not have your suspicions."

"I'm asking, not accusing." Worry, insecurity, and exhaustion caused the words to stick in her throat, but Leah pushed forward. She didn't want to worry over this all day. "I'm asking because I didn't know if I should keep your dinner warm or throw it out. I didn't know if I should stay up or go to bed. What am I supposed to do when my husband hitches up the buggy and takes off late at night? Can you tell me that?"

They'd arrived at Annie's, but Adam had stopped their buggy halfway down the lane.

"I don't want to fight again today." He picked up his hat, glanced at her, and resettled the hat on his head. "Please. It's the Lord's Day. I know carrying the twins is difficult—"

"Do not blame this on the *bopplin*."

Adam closed his eyes, and she knew, absolutely knew then he couldn't stand the sight of her. Did he need to shut out the image of her completely?

"Turn around," she said, trying to sound firm, trying to sound like she wanted to spend the entire day at home alone.

"What?" His eyes opened and he gawked at her as if she'd sprouted corn out of the top of her head.

"Turn around. I want to go home."

"*Nein.*"

"Yes. I want to go home."

"Well, you will have to walk because I'm not taking you." When it seemed they would glare at one another until the snow began to fall, Adam added, "You don't always get what you want, and now is not the time to throw a tantrum like a child."

She had been leaning forward, gesturing toward the reins to make her point. At the word *tantrum*, she pulled back as if he had slapped her.

Adam's jaw clenched and he snapped the reins, signalling to their pretty black gelding to continue down the lane. "*Ya.* We'll be staying and you'll act like a happy *fraa*, whether you feel like it or not. I might not be able to satisfy you in any way Leah, but we won't be upsetting our family over this. They have enough worries."

She stared straight ahead as he directed the gelding around the bend and into view of Annie and Samuel's home—a picture-perfect house with two stories. A garden bed neatly cleaned for the winter surrounded the front porch, and to the southwest, tucked behind the house, sat the traditional red barn.

Leah peered ahead. She could barely make out Annie and Samuel walking from the barn to the house, arm in arm like two young people still courting!

Annie, who had married a man over ten years her senior, a widow with a broken heart. Is that why they were still *in lieb*? Because he had suffered so much? And Annie had spent her time away, among the *Englisch*, earning her nursing certificate. It was a career she gave up to come home and nurse her father. That had led to her joining the church. She seemed so content now. Perhaps after her time away, she more fully appreciated being home.

Annie wasn't the only Weaver child who had spent time away on a *rumspringa*. Adam had too, although he'd never spoken of it in detail. Sometimes Leah worried he would rather still be there, where life was easier, where he wouldn't have three additional mouths to provide for.

Adam brought the buggy to a stop near the back door. When Samuel heard them, he turned with a smile, to help her out. For a moment, a fleeting second or less, she thought something passed between Samuel and her husband. It seemed they shared a look of concern, for the smile almost slipped off Samuel's face. Or she could have imagined it.

Because then he was at her side of the buggy, helping her down, smiling and laughing as he accepted the casserole dish from Adam and helped her into the house. Pretending, as they were, there wasn't a thing in the world wrong.

<hr />

Leah tried not to grimace as she set her huckleberry pudding on the kitchen counter. Her dish was so small and insignificant among all the others. A sigh escaped before she could stop it, but Annie seemed not to notice, or pretended not to notice.

"Berry pudding? Are these from the patch in your south field?"

"They are. We put them up in the summer, and I made the pudding after we got home from town yesterday."

"You should have rested. I know everyone will love it though." Annie scooted around her, placing her hands on her shoulders as the door opened again and her parents walked inside.

Jacob Weaver's face lit up when he saw her. Leah knew that her father-in-law loved her. There was no faking some things, and the grin on his face was genuine.

"It smells *wunderbaar* in here," he declared as he set his cane by the door and made his way across the room. He still walked with a slight limp from the buggy accident that had happened three years earlier, the disaster that had brought Annie home—and brought Annie and Samuel together. Leah supposed it was a case of what had been meant for evil, God had used for good.

Thinking back to that time caused her heart to ache.

She glanced up and across the room, saw Adam talking to Samuel and laughing at something he said. Things had been so natural between her and him then—before they wed, before the babies. She'd spent months looking forward to being a wife and a mother. Now she was learning that sometimes life was nothing like what you expected.

"You're looking very *gut*. Both of you are." Jacob hugged first Leah and then Annie. "How are my favorite girls?"

"*Dat*. I thought you said I was your favorite girl." Reba stuck her bottom lip out in a pout as she set a plate of cold chicken on the counter.

She was still tall and awfully thin for a seventeen-year-old girl, but any outside markings of a tomboy were gone. Now the quietness and beauty about her was hard to ignore. Leah had noticed how she'd changed at church meeting last week. When Reba walked by a group of older boys, they had stopped talking and stared after her, as if she were new to their community. One had shaken his head and blushed all the way to the rim of his hat.

Reba, in keeping with her natural inclination to be clueless around two-footed beasts, had seemed oblivious.

"Didn't you?" Reba teased, sneaking a piece of cheese from one of the plates. "Tell Annie you did call me your favorite last night."

"*Ya*. I suppose I did," Jacob admitted. "Just now I meant she and Leah are my favorite older girls."

Reba laughed and moved to the living room, where she proceeded to corner Samuel. Leah heard the words *poultice* and *herbs* then *mare*. Samuel walked over to a shelf of books, selected one, and handed it to her.

The room filled with conversation as Charity described her latest buggy ride with David Hostetler and Rebekah remarked on the pudding Leah had brought.

The back door opened again and the gusting winter wind nearly tugged it out of *Onkel* Eli's hand. *Onkel* Eli, Jacob's brother, stepped inside with Rachel. She had apparently accepted a ride with Eli, though Annie confessed she had feared Rachel would change her mind and not come. After having been married to Adam over two years, Leah felt as if she knew Eli well, but she couldn't have told anyone a lot of details about him. He was one of those people you seemed to have known all your life, and she probably had. He'd lived in their district for as long as she could remember, but she'd been a child and he'd been an adult.

After she'd joined the Weaver family, he'd become her *onkel*—plain and simple. He'd accepted her as if she'd always been part of the family. She still didn't actually know anything about him though. He was merely *Onkel* Eli—a sweet old guy who loved to make toys, nearly always had a twinkle in his eyes, and didn't seem to have a harsh bone in his body. She wondered for a moment if he could fix the problems in a marriage, if maybe she should go and talk to him next week.

That was ridiculous though. He'd never been in a relationship as far as she knew! She pushed the thought away.

Eli wasn't as old as she had at first thought—maybe in his early forties. When she'd once asked Adam why he'd never married, Adam had shrugged and said, "Maybe he never met the right gal."

The right gal was certainly not standing next to him, removing her coat. Rachel Zook might still be beautiful, and she couldn't be over thirty, but she was not marriage material. How old was she? Leah would never even think of asking. She wasn't exactly scared of her, but she wasn't foolish either. Rachel had the prettiest skin of any woman she'd ever known, other than maybe the *Englisch* movie stars, and Leah hadn't known any of them personally. She had seen them on the front of magazines as she waited in line to check out at the larger discount store.

But the frown on Rachel's face—it seemed carved there.

Today she wore her customary gray dress and black apron. Did she ever wear anything else? And why? Was she still in mourning for her husband, who had passed three years ago?

All these thoughts flitted through Leah's mind in the time it took Eli and Rachel to walk into the room. Rachel's two boys tumbled in from the cold, but Leah barely had time to focus on them. Her attention was completely on Eli, who made no attempt to conceal his argument with Rachel.

"'Course I can read." He took off his hat and knocked it against his pants leg, as if it had snow on it, which it didn't. Eli was tall and had managed to keep fit though he had no fields to speak of, but rather a small garden. His light brown hair had a tinge of gray to it, and he sported no beard since he'd never been married. Around his eyes a few wrinkles were beginning to show, but who noticed? He had the kindest, bluest eyes Leah had ever seen.

"You seem confused."

"I am confused." He didn't move out of the doorway, and Rachel had to nudge him a little so she could close the door.

She let out a sigh and shook her head. "I don't have time for this. What exactly is your problem?"

"My problem is that you've doubled the cost of the toys I sell at the store. People won't pay that much."

"Of course they will. It's ridiculous, but they will because it's Amish woodwork. I'm running a business, Eli." She stopped and looked around as if she were seeing the group for the first time. Everyone had fallen silent.

"I tell you they won't, and I didn't make those toys so they could sit on a shelf. I made them for children."

"Eli, those are the prices I've decided on. Leave them in the store or take them somewhere else."

"Where?"

"Not my problem." Rachel turned around, searching the room for her boys, content when she saw them seated at the checkerboard.

"That's all you have to say? It's not your problem?" Eli's voice rose in frustration.

"It's not."

Jacob cleared his throat and limped toward them. "Perhaps today isn't the proper time to be discussing business matters—"

"One moment, Jacob." Eli turned back to Rachel. "Bontrager never raised my prices without consulting me."

"As you're aware, Bontrager doesn't own the store anymore. I own the store."

"What if I take a smaller commission and you return the prices to what they were previously?"

Rachel closed her eyes. "I fail to see what difference it makes to you. Your profit will remain the same—"

"It does make a difference, because I tell you they won't sell."

"They will, and I needed to change my price structure for business purposes, which I don't expect you to be able to understand." Her hand came out and she dismissed him with a wave as she turned toward the main part of the room. "Trust me when I say *Englischers* will buy anything I hang a *Made by Amish* sign in front of. They're even buying those horrid knitted booties Leah makes."

Eli gaped at her, but Rachel didn't notice. She was searching the room for Leah. "There you are. Leah, I need more of your knitted booties if you've managed to finish any."

Leah's mouth opened, though she was too stunned to say anything. Fortunately, she didn't have to, because at that point Adam stepped forward.

6

When Adam stepped forward, he knew it was a bad idea.

Samuel's hand on his arm told him it was a bad idea. Then there was that tingling sensation on his scalp. His mother used to call that his good angel. Adam wasn't so sure he had a good angel anymore, not the way things had been going.

But he was certain about one thing.

"There's no need to insult Leah," he said.

"Did I insult her?" Rachel looked at him in surprise.

"You did. You were rude to her a moment ago when you referred to her knitting as horrid. She works very hard on those booties you make a profit on, and if you don't want them you should say so—"

"Oh my goodness." Rachel threw up her hands in exasperation. "I believe I asked her for more."

"You owe her an apology," Adam insisted.

"For what?"

"For what you said to my *fraa*."

Rachel clamped her mouth shut, but she did have the good grace to blush.

"Adam, perhaps you could allow me to have a word with my *schweschder*."

Interesting that Samuel used that term. It had the desired effect, causing Adam to pull in a deep breath and step back.

He understood Rachel was Mary's sister—she was Samuel's sister-in-law, but that didn't give her the right to come into the midst of their family and act rudely. It didn't give her the right to disregard his wife's feelings.

"Adam, let's you and I step outside for a moment." Jacob's tone indicated it was an order, not a request, so Adam snatched his coat off the hook by the door, along with his hat, and stormed out ahead of his father. The last two things he saw before stepping out into the cold were Samuel leading Rachel into the front guest room and Leah standing in the kitchen.

Leah, with a smile playing on her face.

Now what was she looking so pleased about? And how long had it been since he'd done anything to make her happy? She'd been stewing over their fight in the buggy since they'd arrived.

⁂

Adam made it to Samuel's barn before he realized his dad was having trouble keeping up with his long, angry strides. Correction—Jacob wasn't even attempting to keep up with him. As usual, Jacob went at his own pace.

He even paused to gaze up into the limbs of a forty-foot red maple to the east of Samuel's barn.

"You're going to freeze out here, *dat*. The weather's turning. Come into the barn."

Jacob appeared not to hear. He pointed up at the brilliant red and orange leaves with his cane. "Never ceases to amaze me, these colors."

"It's only a tree. Leaves turn every year." Adam realized he sounded like a stubborn child, but he couldn't stop himself. He'd worked on the handsaw until late into the night. It had not gone back together as easily as he'd predicted, especially after he'd broken one of the parts in the small engine. Fortunately, the part he'd picked up in town at the hardware store—the part he'd left at eight-thirty to purchase—had worked, once he'd finally put the machine back together correctly.

"True. You're right, but the fact it happens every year doesn't make it less of a miracle." Jacob turned and looked at him then, raised an eyebrow, and joined him at the door to the barn. "Same is true with Leah's *bopplin*, Son. *Kinner* are born every year, every day of every year, but it's still a miracle they are—a true miracle of *Gotte*."

"I know, *Dat*. Miracle—got it." Adam walked over to an upended milking pail and sat on it. "I suspect that isn't what you wanted to talk to me about."

Jacob sat on the wooden crate next to him, so they were both staring down the length of Samuel's barn. It wasn't an overly large barn, and Samuel used a portion of it for seeing patients, so barely half of it contained animals. Adam could see everything was well tended though. The familiar smells and sounds eased some of the tension in his shoulders. How long had it taken Samuel to set things just so? How long had Samuel owned this place? And how had he survived the years alone, the years after Mary and his child had died?

A shiver passed through Adam's heart, but he pushed it away. He focused instead on what had happened back in the house. "Rachel was in the wrong, and you know it."

"*Ya*, maybe you're right."

"She shouldn't have been rude. Leah is having a difficult enough time."

"Why is that?"

Adam's train of thought slammed to a stop. He'd been making a list of Rachel's wrongs, ready to rattle them off to his father, ready to tick them off on the fingers of his left hand. "Why is what?"

"Why is Leah having a difficult time?"

"Let's not make this about Leah."

Jacob squinted at him and waited, resting his hand against the top of his cane and stretching his leg, his right leg that had never healed as well as the other, out in front of him.

"It's not about Leah," Adam repeated. "It's about Rachel and her behavior."

Silence settled around them, until Adam became aware of the horses in the stalls, the wind against the side of the barn, and the grumbling in his stomach.

Finally, he took off his hat and scrubbed his hand through his hair. "I don't know what you want to talk to me about. I don't even know why we're out here when we could be inside eating Sunday dinner."

Jacob nodded, as if that made sense. Slowly he moved his fingers down the length of his cane and studied the grain of the wood. When he began speaking, there was no condemnation in his voice, and perhaps that's why Adam was able to listen to what he had to say.

"Everyone in your *schweschder's* house knows that Rachel acted inappropriately, but maybe we don't know why. Sometimes, Adam, a thing is broken in a person, much as the bone was broken in my leg. The doctors were able to fix my leg." He tapped his shin with the cane, and something inside of Adam flinched.

He remembered too well the fear his father might not have survived the buggy accident and the deathly whiteness of Jacob's face when they had found him in the snow that evening. Samuel had been the first to spy the twisted buggy, but

Adam had joined them there as they'd waited for the ambulance. It had been a frightening time and perhaps when he'd first stepped into manhood.

"When a thing is broken inside a person, way down deep inside, it can become infected. It can affect everything else— like the infection in my leg affected my entire body. Like the dirt in the engines you fix affect the entire machine. Until the person allows the Lord to see their deepest needs, their deepest fears, they're likely to limp along." This time Jacob reached down and rubbed at his leg, and Adam wondered if it hurt. His father wasn't one to complain, so he'd probably never know. "Fears and needs cause folks to limp along emotionally, much like my leg forces me to hobble."

Adam stood and began pacing. "So you're saying I should allow her to talk to Leah that way, that I shouldn't have defended my *fraa*."

"Kindness is a language which the deaf can hear and the blind can see."

"Rachel is neither deaf nor blind. You're telling me to be kind to her, but the woman is bitter and I will not have her being rude to Leah. At the very least, given Leah's condition, Rachel should treat her with respect—"

"Do you?"

Adam froze, midway to the wall of the barn, pivoted, and stared at his father. "What?"

"Do you treat Leah with respect?"

"Why would you ask me that?"

"It seems you're quite worried about her when someone else acts unkindly, but perhaps you have forgotten your first job as her husband is to love her as Christ loved the church." Jacob didn't blink, didn't back down.

For a moment, Adam thought the sadness in his father's eyes might have something to do with his marriage, but that was crazy. It wasn't as if Jacob could have heard their fighting on the way over, or as if he could know they no longer slept together. Surely those things were normal for a couple in their situation.

Had Leah talked to his father or mother?

And beneath that, quieter, the question his father asked echoed, *Did he treat Leah with respect?*

Reba bounded into the barn. "*Mamm* says the food is ready to eat if you two have finished out here."

"I'm starved, and I imagine your *bruder* is too." Jacob stood and smiled when Reba linked her arm through his.

He made it to the barn door before he turned and said, "You're coming, right?"

Adam nodded, but he didn't follow immediately. He needed a few minutes alone, and suddenly eating wasn't the most important thing on his mind.

<hr>

Annie waited as long as she could, but when her mother sent Reba to the barn to fetch Adam and her father, she knew it was time.

"I'll go and check on Samuel and Rachel."

Rebekah patted her arm. "*Gut*, dear. You tell them the food is ready."

She would have knocked on the guest room door, but Samuel had left it ajar, so she pushed it open, clearing her throat to signal she was walking in. She didn't want to interrupt a private moment between brother and sister-in-law. This was all so awkward. Before they were married, Samuel had shared with her that Rachel had suggested he move back to Ohio. Move there, marry her, and help to raise his nephews.

He might have done it too, out of a sense of obligation, but he'd fallen in love with the community nurse.

"Rachel, I want you to listen to me—"

But she wasn't listening. She was standing with her back to him, looking out the window at the clouds pressing down over their pasture. He reached for her arm and turned her around, and that was when she noticed Annie had entered the room.

"Annie. Have you been listening for long?"

"*Nein*, Rachel. I haven't. *Mamm* asked me to come and tell you the food is ready."

"And so you decided to sneak in here and eavesdrop?"

Samuel let out a sigh of exasperation. His gaze met Annie's and somehow she knew what he wanted. She crossed the room, and instead of joining him, she went to Rachel.

She stood close, but not too close. In the years since Rachel had moved to Mifflin County, Annie had attempted to befriend her. She had failed. Now it seemed to her that Rachel was acting like one of Reba's animals—cornered and frightened. At the same time, the memory of the scene in the next room was fresh. She didn't want anything to hurt or upset Leah or the babies she was carrying.

"Rachel, is there something you need? Something that Samuel and I can do for you? If the store isn't making enough money, we'd be happy to—"

"To do what, Annie? Hold an auction for me? Make me your next charity case?" Rachel stiffened her spine. "That won't be necessary, *danki*."

"You are important to me, Rachel. I think you know that." Samuel scrubbed his hand over his face, and it dawned on Annie how much weight he carried on his shoulders. They'd spoken of this as they lingered over their Bible study earlier. Samuel had confessed some days he did a better job than others of handing his burdens over to their Lord. They'd laughed at the time, admitting their failures. Now she understood that the failing, for both of them, could be a costly one.

"I will, we both will, gladly do what we can to help you—" Samuel paused and glanced toward the door. "As well as Zeke and Matthew."

Annie noticed that Rachel closed her eyes at the mention of her boys.

"But there are others I care for as well. Annie, of course." Their eyes met again, and Annie thought she felt the baby inside of her move. "As well as Annie's family. Leah is young and at a vulnerable time in her pregnancy right now. I consider her to be my family as well as one of my patients."

Samuel stepped closer and lowered his voice. "You will not speak rudely to her again. You will not devalue her in any way. If you have a difference of opinion with Eli, or any business matter that needs settling, you will save it—"

"But he—"

"You will save it for the proper time and place, which is not my home or any home on Sunday."

Rachel's face blushed red.

"Am I clear?"

Rachel drew herself up to her full height, and Annie was struck again by how tall she was, tall and exceptionally beautiful.

"Tell me you understand, Rachel."

She pressed her lips together until they formed a white line. "Oh, I understand."

He motioned, a ladies-first gesture. Rachel left the room, heading straight for the bathroom.

"Do you think she'll be all right?"

"Today? Yes. But something is wrong she's not speaking of. I'll ask the bishop to meet with her, but I doubt she'll be any more open with him. I'll also write her mother." His last words were added softly as he touched her arm gently and they returned to the sitting room.

Jacob and Reba were back from the barn. As they began a time of silent prayer, Adam slipped in through the mudroom. Within a few moments they all began eating and soon they put the rough start to their meal behind them. It wasn't too hard, at least on the surface. Reba entertained them with tales from the veterinary practice. Charity updated them on how David was doing, and Rachel's boys chimed in with stories from the schoolhouse. Soon the snow began to fall outside—not a heavy snowfall, but enough to cast a special glow on the day.

A fire crackled in the big cast-iron stove, and its coziness dispelled any earlier gloom. Eli challenged Matthew to a game of checkers and Jacob sat by the fire, showing Zeke how to whittle a piece of wood into a whistle.

Adam was pretending to read *The Budget*, but it was soon obvious from the sounds behind the paper that he was asleep.

Though Rachel didn't actually participate, she did sit near the window and read.

Leah waddled out of the bathroom and up to the counter as Annie was setting out the desserts. "Little guys must be taking up a lot of room inside me. I can't believe I had to go again."

She glanced from Annie to Rachel, who stood and walked to the other side of the room, to watch Matthew's checkers game.

Annie and Leah were carrying the leftover lunch food to the refrigerator in the mudroom when Leah started giggling.

"Are you going to share with me what you're laughing about?"

"I wish you could have seen the look on your face, and on Samuel's face, when Rachel said my knitted booties were horrid." Leah's giggles turned into full laughs and she had to put her dish down so she could hold her stomach. "Oh my, that was priceless."

"Leah Weaver." Annie lowered her voice to a whisper. "Here I was worried that Rachel Zook had hurt your feelings."

"Didn't hurt my feelings. Doesn't keep her from selling the things I make, and I can use the money. Maybe we can fashion a sign saying *Horrid Little Booties*." Leah giggled again, then wiped her eyes and grew serious as they moved to the window, propped their elbows on the ledge, and studied the falling snow. "And did you see the way Adam jumped to my defense? It was nice."

The silence stretched between them for a few moments.

"My life isn't perfect by any measure," Leah added. "But hers must be awful lonesome."

"Lonesome?"

"Sure. You can be surrounded by people and still be lonesome. No one to speak to once the boys are in bed. No one to watch the snow fall with if you wake early in the morning."

Annie reached forward and touched the windowpane. The temperature outside was dropping, and she was glad she'd be spending the evening beside Samuel. "You're a pretty smart girl, you know that?"

"Doesn't take smartness to understand why someone snaps or to see that Samuel's sister-in-law is afraid of something."

Annie was so surprised at Leah's words that she jerked her head up, bumping it on the window shade that was half pulled down.

Smiling, Leah reached out and straightened Annie's prayer *kapp*.

As they stood there, the sounds of their family in the room behind them, Annie thought about Leah's observation. The idea gained merit the longer she considered it.

"What would Rachel have to be afraid of though?"

"I don't know. Some days I'm afraid of what people will think about me being as big as a house. Other days I'm afraid that my marriage might be broken, and I'm certainly afraid I'm doing things wrong."

Leah's words stayed with Annie as they walked back into the sitting room and helped themselves to a small piece of dessert.

It didn't occur to her until later in the evening that the fight had actually begun with Rachel and Eli. Why would Rachel be picking a fight with Eli?

She'd been so worried about Leah the last few weeks, but now she wondered if maybe Rachel was the one who needed rescuing.

But how did you rescue someone who was afraid, especially when they wouldn't give you even a clue as to what had given them such a fright?

7

Annie spent Monday morning doing the laundry that had piled up from the previous week. Since there was only she and Samuel, there wasn't a lot to do, but she was still surprised at how dirty a man's clothing became when he spent the day working in the fields or in the barn.

She accessed their basement by going outside via the mudroom and down two steps. It had long narrow windows running the length of the south wall. Annie couldn't have explained it, but there was something she liked about the basement. Maybe it was the shelves of food—canned and winking at her along the north wall.

To the left were rows of vegetables—squash, beans, carrots, corn, and peas. They all waited there for her to choose from each evening. It was like having her own grocery store, and though the canning had been hard work, she loved walking downstairs and selecting one for their dinner. The right side of the shelves held berries from Leah's bushes and preserves Annie had made with her mother. There were other fruits as well. Items she'd traded with women from church.

There was abundance.

Every time she came into the basement, to fetch one of the jars or to do the laundry, she was reminded of the harvest and of God's goodness. The words she'd read with Samuel the day before echoed through her mind. "I will cure them, and will reveal unto them the abundance of peace and truth." It was from the book of Jeremiah, from the Old Testament. Jeremiah was one of her favorite books, though there was much violence within its pages. What she clung to were the promises there, despite what Jeremiah and God's people endured.

The jars of food, the windows with the light, even the smell of washing powder—all of it combined to make the basement a cheery place. So even when she came down to do the loads of laundry, Annie found she was in a good mood. She was grateful.

Although it was cold outside, the snow had stopped and the temperatures were above freezing. She'd try hanging the clothes out on the line and see if they'd dry. They probably would.

She filled the machine with two small buckets of hot water, tapped from the water heater, which was a wood-burning one—same as her parents had. Samuel always checked the room on Mondays and made sure everything was ready for her before he went to the barn. Actually, the basement was almost warm, given the water heater, the windows, and the size of the room—about the length and width of their living room.

After measuring a half-cup of laundry powder, Annie pushed their bed sheets into the machine. One yank on the starting cord was enough. The gasoline engine had been stalling, but Adam had come by and serviced it a month ago. This time it started up immediately. She added the soap powder to the water as the agitator began moving the sheets back and forth. Annie glanced at the battery-powered clock on the wall, noting when ten minutes would be up.

A large sink was positioned under the south wall with a cold-water faucet. Next she went through the process of filling both washtubs with rinse water using a small bucket. One she added fabric softener to and the other she added bleach to. By the time she had both of the washtubs ready, the ten minutes were up and she began running the sheets through the wringer and into the first tub of rinse water.

It took several times through to work all the soap out, but in the end their sheets smelled fresh. This was her third and final load for the day. The first two loads sat by the door, waiting for her to carry them outside.

After she'd moved the sheets to her basket, she wrapped up in her coat and scarf and carried the basket outside. In the summer, she would have combined all three loads into one basket, but Samuel had cautioned her about carrying lighter loads—because of the baby. She didn't think wet laundry weighed so much, but caution was a good thing.

As she walked over to the clothesline, the sun was fighting through the high clouds, and she was certain everything would be dry by afternoon. She could hang things in the basement, but preferred the freshness of laundry hung outside.

She was pinning the second sheet to the line when Samuel appeared at her side. "Ready for me to dump your rinse water?"

"*Ya*. How do you always know when I'm done with a load?"

She smiled and slapped at his hand as he reached for the other end of the sheets. "Don't think about it, Samuel. Those sheets took me thirty minutes to clean. Let me see your hands."

"Maybe I'll empty that water for you," he said with a wink.

"*Danki*," she called after him.

He waved as he moved toward the basement. Watching Samuel dump out the water from her washtubs, then stack them back inside the basement, Annie wanted to make him something special for lunch.

And she wanted Leah and Adam to experience the home life she had. She wanted life to always be like this.

It would seem that Adam was feeling he couldn't measure up as a father. And Leah felt unloved or unlovable as a wife. What were they going to do with those two? Or maybe, as Samuel had suggested, it wasn't their place to do anything.

Maybe they were to pray and be the best family they could be. She continued pinning the sheets as her mind replayed their conversation from the night before, after everyone had left, when she heard a buggy approaching. Peeking around the sheets, she saw her sister, Charity, smiling and waving from her buggy.

Samuel came back out of the barn to see to her buggy, and Charity met her at the basement door as she was going back for the other two loads of laundry.

"Let me help you with that."

"I'm sure you didn't come to help me hang clothes," Annie teased.

"Actually I did. I was hoping to make it here before you finished." She ducked inside with Annie and they both came out carrying a basket. They had the rest of the clothes hung in five minutes.

Annie enjoyed watching Charity. She hadn't changed at all in the last three years. Still slightly round and still completely beautiful. She seemed to grow more like their mother every day, both in how she looked and in her temperament. Annie was expecting an announcement that Charity and David Hostetler were to be married, but so far nothing.

Maybe today.

Maybe it was what Charity had come to talk to her about.

They hurried into the kitchen, out of the cold.

"Tell me the real reason you stopped by." Annie began pulling out the leftover stew from a few days before and put water on the stove so she could make them a hot drink.

"I did want to help you with the laundry. I would have been here earlier, but Reba's clothing was a real mess. You wouldn't believe what her dresses look like after a day at the vet clinic."

"Worse than the barn?"

"*Ya.* Much worse."

Annie thought back to the evening she had helped birth the calf. "I suppose I can imagine. Is she working again today?"

"Every weekday and two Saturdays a month. But when she works on a Saturday, Trevor gives her Monday off." Charity wriggled an eyebrow as she buttered four pieces of bread, then slid them onto a pan to place in the oven with the stew.

"Why the look?"

"You know why."

"Tell me Reba isn't sweet on Trevor."

Charity sat down at the table and began flipping through Annie's latest book from the library.

"You know you're not interested in reading that. Now talk to me."

"I'm not sure about Reba. I thought maybe she talked to you yesterday." Charity pushed her *kapp* strings back behind her shoulders.

"*Nein.* She did speak with Samuel about some ointment for a horse."

"Our little *schweschder* is hard to figure sometimes. The moment you think she has eyes for nothing except the four-legged kind, you'll find a note in her dress pocket."

"You're kidding!"

Charity smiled, pulled a folded note from her apron, and slid it across the table. "Not that I've read it."

Annie sat down and stared at the folded note with Reba's name on top. "I'm impressed. You showed real restraint. How do you know it's from Trevor?"

"If you hold it up to the light, you can see his signature."

Annie shook her head and pushed the note back across the table. "And what are you going to do with it?"

"Place it on top of her folded clothes. Maybe if she knows I saw it, she'll spill." Charity laughed.

"This could be a serious matter. Trevor's *Englisch*. What did *mamm* say?"

"She said *Gotte* has his eye on Reba and not to worry about her."

"Sounds like *mamm*." Annie jumped up when she heard the water on the stove begin to boil. "Tea?"

"*Ya*."

"So what about you and David? I thought you might bring up the subject yesterday."

They spent the next twenty minutes talking about David. He was still living with his parents, still working their farm and working a part-time job in town. He and Charity were regularly attending the singings together, and it seemed to her he might be getting serious. He'd kissed her twice.

They hadn't talked about marrying yet.

They had talked about the price of farms, which was high. And twice he'd shown her ads in *The Budget*, ads for dairy farms in Wisconsin. Charity confessed the thought of moving made her stomach hurt and excited her at the same time.

After they shared lunch with Samuel, she walked Charity out to her buggy.

"Any word on Mattie and Jesse?"

"The bypass surgery was a success, and members of their family have taken turns sitting with him so Mattie could come home in the evening."

"*Gut*. So he'll recover fully?"

"The doctors say he should—if he'll follow their directions."

"Exercise, eat healthy, and watch your cholesterol." Charity reached out and hugged Annie. "Don't look so surprised. You've lectured us all."

"Sure you won't stay and quilt with me?"

"*Nein*. I have my own projects at home. *Mamm* went to Leah's to help with the laundry first thing this morning. I want to get home and hear how she's doing."

"She seemed better by the time they left yesterday." Annie hugged her again, then stood back as Charity picked up her mare's reins.

She was pleased her mother had gone to Leah and Adam's this morning. Pleased they lived close enough to help one another. Although Leah and Adam were having a tough spell perhaps it would make them stronger in the end.

Each family was different, and she would need to trust that Leah and Adam would find their way. But perhaps a word here or there would help. Maybe she could speak with Adam and nudge things along. After all, who knew her brother better than she did?

In the meantime, she would work on the quilt.

She had the rest of the afternoon to piece together her sample square. She'd neglected to do that once, on a quilt she was making for auction. She'd been making an Amish basket quilt and thought she was experienced enough to bypass the step.

Walking up to her sewing room, she thought back on how she had certainly learned her lesson that year. The basket quilt had been a disaster. It had taken all of her mother's skill to help her fix it, and in the end, she'd needed to repurchase part of the fabric. All because she hadn't made a sample square.

A costly mistake but one she'd never repeated. Every quilt she'd done since, she had taken the time to complete this step.

Which was where she'd begin this afternoon. Surprisingly, she wasn't the least bit sleepy—perhaps the napping phase of her pregnancy had passed. Glancing out the window, she could see their sheets snapping in the light wind. Samuel was walking toward the house, and more clouds were rolling in. Maybe they'd have snow again by evening, and this time it might be more than a mere dusting.

Fine with her. She had finished the laundry and had the entire afternoon to work on Leah's quilt. While she sewed, she'd pray for the babies and for Leah and Adam. She'd complete the sample square, then once that was done, the rest of the quilt should be easy work.

Perhaps God would present an opportunity for her to speak with her brother. If she didn't hear from Adam or Leah before Wednesday, she'd take them a meal when Samuel went to town. He wanted to see to some repairs around Rachel's place and it would give her a chance to spend time with Leah.

Provided they didn't have any other medical emergencies.

8

Monday evening—or was it in the wee hours of Tuesday morning?—Leah woke to a room so dark she couldn't see the opposite wall. She lay there for a few minutes and tried to convince herself she wasn't completely awake, but it was no use pretending. When her thoughts turned to how Rebekah had helped her with the wash, how nice it had been not to spend the day alone, she knew she was wide awake.

She tried to turn over on her side, but the giant beach ball that had become her stomach wouldn't allow her to. She lay in the darkness, determined to go back to sleep, but her mind refused to quiet. Instead, she listened to every sound—the branches of the eastern white pine tree against their room, the sound of the wind outside the window, even a night bird calling out to its mate.

Was it still snowing?

How much had accumulated?

What time was it anyway?

If she wiggled and worked at it, she might be able to roll over and see the clock on her nightstand. Adam had bought her the small ivory-colored, battery-operated clock for her birthday. He'd laughed, but he'd bought it. She'd pointed it out to him at the store—a week before she'd turned twenty-two.

"And who needs a clock in the bedroom?" he'd asked. "We've never had one before."

"I know, but it would be nice to know how long the babies have slept or if I should check on them."

"The babies will be waking you when it's time to feed them again. You won't need a clock for that."

But he'd gone back to the store while she was visiting at the cafe with Rebekah, and later he'd wrapped up the very one she'd shown him. He'd even put a bow on the package and set it on the kitchen table so that it was the first thing she'd seen the morning of her birthday. When she thought of that morning, it seemed like she was remembering something in one of the books Annie liked to read or something that happened to someone else.

Too bad she couldn't crane her neck around and see the clock. Maybe she could sit up without waking Adam. She'd never get back to sleep now anyway. The pressure in her back felt like the time she'd scrubbed all the floors in a single day. It almost felt as if someone had their hands on her back and was pushing.

Leah pushed the covers off her stomach, careful not to disturb Adam, which was when she realized he wasn't even in bed. Was it not as late as she thought? Or had he moved to the couch again?

She rotated her legs around to the floor and used her arms to push herself into a sitting position. Reaching for the clock, she tapped the button on top and the light gently glowed, revealing the time—ten minutes after three.

Adam had definitely moved to the couch.

He slept there more than he did in their own bed.

Was it because her tossing kept him awake?

Sleeping with her must be like sleeping in a rocking buggy. She wiggled and turned and couldn't be still for more than a few moments. Lying in any single position had become too uncomfortable. She'd known pregnancies could be hard, and she'd heard the horror stories about stretch marks and not being able to see one's feet. Nothing had prepared her for this though. The constant worry, the aches, the not sleeping . . . those were things no one talked about.

And she hadn't felt her husband's arms around her in months. Not that his arms would fit around her. Not that he would want to put his arms around her even if he could.

She was whining.

She hadn't opened her mouth, and Adam was still asleep, but she was whining nonetheless. Watching Annie with Samuel on Sunday had reminded her of how she used to be with Adam—she used to be nicer. Standing, she waited a moment to be sure she was balanced. Wouldn't do to fall over in her own bedroom. Then she'd be a whining wife and a troublesome one, too.

Waddling to the bathroom, she vowed to stop and change her attitude. Twenty-two was much too young to turn into a whiner, plus she didn't want to be that kind of wife or mother. Her husband would avoid her, and her children would hide in the barn with their father.

One more thing to worry about.

She shut the door to the bathroom as quietly as possible. Reaching for the small flashlight they kept on the counter near the sink, she flipped it on. It did nothing to alleviate the pain pulsating in her lower back, but at least she could see what she was doing. She took care of her bathroom needs, and glanced into the small mirror while she rinsed her hands at the sink. With her hair down she almost looked like the young woman who had married Adam—the young woman she still felt like sometimes, on the inside.

She combed her fingers through her blonde hair, which reached well past her waist. Adam used to say her hair reminded him of the wheat in the fields—silky, golden, and precious. With a sigh, she pulled her hair behind her shoulders. If she did have a girl, she would brush her hair every night. The thought made her smile; after all, no one carried a baby forever. She was turning to go back into their bedroom when a pain rippled across her stomach. Leah rubbed one hand over the top of her protruding belly and her other hand over the bottom.

"It's only the false labor," she murmured, but then another pain claimed her and she sank to the floor. Placing her head against the rug, she focused on breathing in and out and tried to calm her racing heart. She could wake Adam, but probably it was the practice pains, same as two nights ago.

He needed his rest. He worked so hard that he'd fallen asleep reading the paper on Sunday.

Suddenly she needed to go to the bathroom again, needed to go badly, but she didn't think she could stand. Reaching for the cabinet, she tried to pull herself up and that was when the pressure from the babies increased. That was when she knew this was nothing like two nights ago.

Adam had wakened when Leah turned the small flashlight on in the bathroom. He had wanted to go to her immediately, but it was probably better if he didn't. These days she seemed to prefer her privacy.

He lay in the sitting room, and stared up at the ceiling. When he'd built the small, snug house, he had never dreamed he'd be spending so many nights sleeping on the couch! He rolled to his side and punched his pillow. If he was uncomfortable, how did Leah feel? How did she even manage to stand or sit?

He didn't understand how anyone could abide changing their shape so much. His mother had her last baby when he was six, his youngest sister, Reba. He could barely remember, but he'd seen plenty of pregnant women in his life. When Annie had come home from the city, that first winter, he'd driven her to more than one birthing in the middle of the night. Most of the time, he'd been able to hide out in the barn while the women endured their labor, but occasionally he'd had to stay in the house. He would never forget those nights.

But this wasn't like those nights.

It wasn't time for his children to be born.

And Leah was nothing like those women. Leah was so large that when they stood together, they were still a foot apart! It would be funny if he didn't miss her so much.

Flipping over onto his back, he wondered again if he should go and check on her. She'd been in the bathroom for a good five minutes. He'd wait a little while longer and then he'd go and knock. When they'd first married, she'd never shut the door, but now shut doors were standard procedure.

He thought back on what Samuel had said on Saturday. "Leah needs to know you love her."

Of course, he loved her! Didn't he work all the time? When he wasn't tending to their animals or working on the barn, he was preparing the fields and reading up on ways to produce more crops on their small amount of land. Then there was the work on the engines.

Adam tossed over to his side, staring into the darkness at the back of the couch.

The engines were the answer. His land could only produce so much, but people always needed their small engines repaired. If he could build up a good client base, then he'd have steady income all year long. Then his wife and children would have no need to worry.

"Leah needs to know you love her."

He wanted to go to her. Why was she still in the bathroom? He sat up and stared at the closed door. One more minute. It was all he was waiting.

He'd been short-tempered lately and he felt bad about that. His father was right—it wasn't respectful. He'd spoken to Leah harshly on the way to the luncheon Sunday and he should apologize. Middle of the night might not be the best time, but then again neither of them were sleeping.

In the old days, before the twins, they'd occasionally wake in the middle of the night and talk. Of course, sometimes they'd do more than talk.

He missed his wife!

Standing up, he walked to the bathroom door and tapped on it lightly.

"Leah, are you all right?"

There was no answer. Maybe she'd fallen asleep in there. He tapped again.

"Leah? Honey? I'm coming in." Pushing the door open, he poked his head through. The flashlight she'd been using was on the floor. It had fallen out of her hand but was still on, and its beam provided enough light for him to see her. Leah lay huddled on the bathroom floor.

She gave no indication she'd heard him enter the room.

He dropped to the floor beside her, pushed her hair—her beautiful blonde hair—back out of her face. He needed to see her. He needed to speak with her.

"Honey. What is it? Talk to me, Leah."

"Adam . . ."

His name on her lips caused his heart to leap. What had he thought? That she'd died there while he'd been tossing on the couch?

"*Was iss letz?*" he whispered, pressing his forehead to hers.

"The babies, Adam."

When he stroked her cheek her eyes fluttered open, but then a shriek clawed its way up and out of her throat. She pulled herself back into a ball, as if she were protecting the children in her womb.

For the first time that night, maybe for the first time in his life, Adam felt terror snake down his spine and take root in his heart.

"I'll move you to the bed."

"*Nein.*"

"You can't stay here . . ."

Again the scream and he couldn't make out her words if there were any. Her hair cascaded down and she was a ball, a world curled in on herself. The floor was cold, but Adam had begun sweating like his workhorses.

For Leah, the pain must have passed because she began to shiver as she reached for his hand and clutched it.

"I'll fetch you a quilt."

"The old one," she murmured.

Her request pushed the fear back. Surely if she could worry about such a thing there was hope. Surely they would see their way through this night. But he had to go for help. He had to put out the call for Belinda and Samuel and Annie.

He was back with the old quilt she kept in the blanket chest, the one that was tattered. He'd heard her say she was going to cut it up for a rag quilt, as soon as the babies arrived and she was able to reach her treadle machine again.

Covering her as another spasm rocked her body, he realized she might be thirsty. He jumped back up, filled the cup they kept near the sink and offered it to her. She raised her head enough to sip a little before cowering back into a ball.

"I'm going to ring the bell, Leah."

"Don't go," she begged.

"To ring the bell. David will hear and come."

"Stay with me." Her voice was broken, pleading.

"Two minutes. It will take me two minutes." He didn't wait. Instead, he kissed her softly on the cheek. How long had it been since he'd done that? Why had he been so remiss?

Then he ran out the door. Forgetting his shoes, forgetting his coat, not pausing to consider he still wore his nightclothes. Forgetting everything but the three lives behind him.

9

Annie woke to the sound of ringing on their baby monitor.

Samuel was already pulling on his clothes. "Try to go back to sleep," he whispered, stopping long enough to brush a kiss on her forehead before heading down the stairs.

Sleeping was impossible though. Instead, she counted the rings on the telephone in their barn. It was a cell phone, and they could have brought it in the house. They'd both met with the bishop and discussed this at length. The reason Bishop Levi had allowed the phone was because she and Samuel were often called upon to help families within their community. The new process seemed to be working well. When someone was sick, a family member would run down to the nearest phone shack, where they would put in a call to Samuel.

Three years ago, they would bypass the phone shack and drive their buggy out to Samuel's home. But too often his answer had been that they should have stopped and placed the 9-1-1 emergency call. Precious moments were lost.

Their people were not slow in understanding what constituted an emergency. They certainly were intelligent enough to know the difference in most cases—to know what Samuel, as an herbalist, could help with, and what required a hospital. Annie had taken a class on homeopathic medicine while earning her nursing certification. She'd been surprised to learn that there was a growing interest among *Englischers* regarding the benefit of natural substances for certain ailments. Of course, others thought it was so much mumbo-jumbo. She wondered what her old co-workers would think, seeing her now.

As Annie stood and began dressing, her mind turned back to the phone and the families in her community. She was certain the majority of those men and women were actually quite intelligent—smart enough to know when to call an ambulance rather than Samuel.

No, the problem seemed to be twofold. First of all, they were slow to change. They based their entire way of life on things staying the way things had always been. Because of that, they were hesitant to call on the *Englisch* for medical assistance, though they would when Samuel told them it was best.

The second problem was less noble in her mind, and caused her to think of the donkeys in their neighbor's pasture. Many of the families in their part of Pennsylvania were stubborn, plain and simple. These families would often argue with Samuel when he told them to call for help. She couldn't begin to imagine what it must be like to live in an old order Amish community. Long before she was born, her community had accepted the use of gas stoves, gas refrigerators, even triangles on the buggies. But going directly to the *Englisch* hospital? That was something few would do.

And so they had sat with Bishop Levi before they'd married and discussed the wisdom of installing a phone. Both she and Samuel had agreed they didn't want it in their home, didn't want it disrupting their lives. Whether it was a cell phone or a landline didn't seem to make much difference. It would be a distraction. In the end, they'd decided on a cell phone, which

Samuel could carry with him when he was on a call. Annie had taken it with her occasionally when she'd had a birthing Belinda couldn't attend. She hadn't had cause to use it, but both she and Samuel remembered the first birth they had assisted together. God had provided direction that night, and it seemed He was providing direction with the bishop's allowance.

So the phone sat in the barn on a special battery charger. Doc Stoltzfus had suggested the baby monitor—also battery-operated, which allowed them to hear it from the house if it rang. Still a distraction, but at least a distant one.

Like tonight.

What time was it?

As she started downstairs, the light from the flashlight she was carrying fell on her quilting bag. She was ready to begin work on the quilt in earnest.

If she needed to leave with Samuel on a home visit, it would be good to take the bag with her. She'd finished her sample square the day before and had even found enough time to recalculate the amount of fabric of each color she would need. Her plan was to use a white for the background of each block, and border them with a nice green. She'd determined the colors for each boy and girl she would appliqué as well as the nine-patch block to separate each square. And she'd written it all down, measured twice, and checked her calculations.

Picking up the bag, she continued to the first floor. She peered out the window and saw a light piercing the darkness. Samuel had opened the barn doors and hitched the buggy. Hurrying, she gathered together what supplies they might need, including both their medical bags and her coat. More snow had fallen while they'd slept.

Shining her flashlight in the direction of the kitchen clock, she was surprised to see it was nearly four. They'd had almost a full night's sleep. That was good. Annie ran her hand over her stomach. It seemed every day now the baby felt bigger and stronger.

She was at the front door holding all of their things when Samuel pulled the buggy alongside the porch. Not waiting for him to exit the buggy, she stepped out into the cold predawn, pulled the door shut behind her, and hurried down their front porch steps.

Slipping into the buggy, she accepted the blanket he handed her. "I brought your medical bag as well as mine, some food you might want to eat on the way, and a little of the milk we had left, though I didn't have time to heat any *kaffi*—"

"Annie."

She was so busy settling into the seat, placing the bags at her feet, and tucking the blanket around her lap she hadn't stopped to study him. In fact, she'd turned off the flashlight as soon as she'd climbed into the buggy. But something in his voice caused her to stop, to hold perfectly still, to steel herself against his next words.

"It's Leah."

"Leah—"

Samuel murmured to Beni, who started off down the lane at a fast clip, as if the mare understood their urgency.

"It's the *bopplin*?" Her voice shook slightly and she cleared her throat, then tried again. "They're coming?"

She couldn't make out his expression, but she could see his profile as her eyes adjusted to the darkness.

"I don't think so. David called and he couldn't give me many details, but it doesn't sound as if her water had broken yet."

"David called?"

"Adam had rung the bell. David hurried over to their place."

"Thank *Gotte* he lives close."

Samuel nodded, reached over, and squeezed her hand. As they approached the two-lane blacktop, he pulled his hand away and focused on directing her mare.

"I told him to call Belinda as soon as he hung up. He rang back before I'd finished hitching up Beni. She's going to meet us there."

Annie nodded, even as she closed her eyes and began to pray.

They travelled another five minutes, the horse's steady gait and Samuel's strong presence calming the panic trying to claim hold. The prayers in her heart soothed the ache for her brother's children.

"Should we call the ambulance, Samuel? Did you bring the phone?"

"*Ya*, I have it, though perhaps it is only false labor—"

"Or prelabor."

"David didn't have many details. He knew her pains were close, but Adam wouldn't come outside to speak to him."

"Where was he?"

"In the bathroom with her. David went into the house and stood speaking to them through the door. Adam said he found her that way, collapsed on the floor."

"Six weeks early. They won't weigh much."

"*Gotte* knows what they weigh, Annie. And he knows the day they're appointed to make their appearance." He reached over and claimed her hand. "We'll go to her and assess her condition."

"And convince her to go to the *Englisch* hospital."

"If she's still having contractions, yes."

Annie stared out the buggy window. The sky still showed no signs of dawn. As her mind went over all that could go wrong, the view outside remained pitch black.

<hr>

Though the pains hadn't lessened, it helped that Adam was still with her. Leah was ashamed she had ever doubted her husband's feelings. Seeing him now, feeling his arms around her as they knelt on the cold floor, she realized how foolish, how childish she had been.

How long had it been since David had gone for help?

How long would this night last?

Another pain rippled across her stomach and she felt Adam's hand on her face, combing her hair away. His voice was a whisper in her ear. It didn't matter what words he was praying, only that he was so close. She fell into a light sleep as soon as the muscles surrounding the babies relaxed. Her last thoughts were of the comfort of the old quilt warming her and the calm assurance she felt wrapped in Adam's strong arms. He'd succeeded in moving her so that his back was to the wall and she lay with her back to him, lay in the circle of his arms.

His voice in her ear.

His lips on her hair.

His arms holding the quilt around her, touching her stomach each time the wave of agony hit again.

It was an intimacy beyond anything they'd ever shared, and it was almost worth her fear she might not survive it.

But women did survive such hours.

Didn't they?

She closed her eyes and fell asleep again. When she opened them, Adam was gone. Someone had slipped a pillow beneath her head. Annie knelt beside her, wiping her brow with a cool cloth.

"Annie, when did you—"

"We've been here a few minutes."

"Adam?"

"He's in the next room, with Samuel. We're going to move you to the bedroom, Leah. Samuel needs to examine you, and it would be difficult here. Your contractions are coming every eight minutes. You should have another soon, then Samuel and Adam will carry you to your bed."

Leah nodded though fear flooded every space of her heart. The tiny bathroom had become her world in the last few hours. Somehow she had reasoned if she could stay here, stay with Adam, everything would turn out all right.

She glanced around and noticed there was more light. A battery-powered lantern sat on the counter, and the beam from two flashlights shone on the ceiling.

"One more minute, dear. It's important you don't push. Hold my hand."

"It's time?" Samuel's voice was calm, low, and she caught a glimpse of him before the wall of pain slammed into her and she squeezed her eyes shut.

"Count, Leah. One, two, three . . ." Samuel's hands were on her stomach, and somehow she heard Adam behind her. Annie continued holding her hand and sponging her forehead with the cool cloth.

They'd barely stopped counting when Adam and Samuel were helping her to her feet.

"I'm not sure that I can—"

"Already done," Annie chirped.

Leah was sure her legs would give away, but she hardly had to use them at all. Samuel and Adam were on either side of her, steadying her and supporting all of her weight between them. As they guided her from the bathroom to her bed, she saw that Annie had pulled back the covers and brought in more lanterns, though now there was a touch of morning light through the windows.

"*Gut*," Samuel declared. "Now Adam, if you'll go out and see to our horse."

"But surely David can do that."

"*Ya*, probably you're right. I think he'd like some of the *kaffi* Annie started when we arrived though. He's had a long night, too."

Leah thought she saw Samuel wink at Annie. What secret joke had passed between them? If they could banter back and forth, her condition must not be as serious as she feared. Some of the worry constricting her heart backed away.

Annie had settled her into the bed, tied back her hair, and given her a drink of water.

"Can you take Leah's vitals again?" Samuel asked.

"Sure thing." Annie fastened the black material over Leah's left arm and pumped up the blood pressure cuff. "Long night?"

"*Ya*. At first I thought it was the practice labor."

"Maybe it is." Annie noted her blood pressure on a pad of paper, then relayed the numbers to Samuel, who was prepping to examine her.

"Let's see how close these *bopplin* are to coming."

The exam was quick. Samuel was done well before the next contraction hit. Leah could tell by the look on Samuel's face this was not another case of pre-labor, but then she'd known that the moment she collapsed on the bathroom floor.

Annie covered her with the quilt, offered her another drink of water, and they prepared for the next contraction. It was ending as Adam entered the room.

Samuel wasted no time getting to the point. "I'd like to use the phone I carry to call an ambulance."

"But Annie said Belinda is coming—" Leah ran her hand over the stitching of her quilt, the wedding quilt she'd made for her and Adam. She remembered working on it at her mother's house.

"She'll be here soon, but she will say the same thing." Samuel moved from the foot of the bed to stand next to her. "Every moment we wait is a moment lost. Your vitals are good and the heartbeats of your *bopplin* are strong, but you've begun to dilate. We need to stop your labor before it progresses any further. Contractions are stressful on the *bopplin*, and we don't want them to enter the birth canal."

"You haven't lost your water yet, Leah." Annie kept her voice calm, making sure Leah and Adam looked at her before she continued. "The paramedics will be able to start an IV with a bolus solution in case you are dehydrated. Once you arrive at the hospital, the doctors will add medication to your IV if it's necessary. Both should help postpone your labor."

Adam sank into a chair next to the bed. "Then why does she have to go to the hospital?"

"A paramedic can't give magnesium, which Leah may need to stop her labor. Plus she needs to be monitored closely for at least a few days."

"How many days?" Leah felt her heart rate kick up a notch. She'd never been away from home before.

"There's no way to know." Annie patted her arm.

"I don't understand," Adam said. "Maybe it will stop like before."

"Leah's contractions are steady and increasing in length. Also her cervix has begun to dilate," Samuel explained. "This is definitely not false labor."

"Isn't there an herb you can give her to stop her labor?"

"No. There isn't. The doctors at the hospital have the correct medicine. You can trust them, Adam."

"But if it's time for the *bopplin* to be born—"

Time for the babies? It wasn't even Thanksgiving yet. The babies were due at Christmas. Tears welled up in Leah's eyes and threatened to spill over. Annie kept checking her watch, which was when Leah realized another contraction was due any minute.

"If it's *Gotte's wille*, then they will be," Samuel agreed. "But every day we can give them in Leah's womb is an extra day they have to gain weight, an extra day for their lungs to develop. It's very important we give them that time."

Adam continued to shake his head. "We knew there was a possibility we'd have to go to the hospital, but what you're talking about is different. I want to do what's best for Leah and for the babies. How long would she be there?"

"I don't know. As long as it takes." Samuel scrubbed his hand over his face. "I'll speak plainly. We need to give them every chance we can. If they're born tonight, they will have a difficult fight ahead of them. Their lungs might be underdeveloped and their birth weight will be low. Plus, I can't assist that kind of birth here. Belinda can't either."

Adam reached for Leah's hand and kissed it gently. She realized at that moment how difficult this must be for him. How could she comfort him?

"Everything will be fine, Adam." She searched her heart for confidence she didn't feel. What was it they had read in their Bible on Sunday? Not to worry, and about the flowers of the field. "Remember the verses you chose on Sunday? How God cares for us more than the flowers?"

"From Luke. *Ya.*"

"If Samuel says we should go now, then we should go. *Gotte* has sent him to our community for this reason, because he knows what is best. The rest we shouldn't worry about."

"*Ya.* Okay. I know you're both right." Adam stared at her, then up at Annie. "Will you go with us?"

"Of course."

"Then place the call."

As Samuel was pulling out the phone, the next contraction finally hit. Adam and Annie helped Leah through it. This time instead of counting, she focused on an image of lilies.

10

Adam actually flinched when the paramedic shut the back doors to the ambulance. His *fraa* was inside, not to mention his children.

"Annie's with her," Samuel reminded him.

"You'll be mere moments behind," David added. His hair looked as if he'd fallen asleep in the barn at some point.

Nodding, Adam kept his eyes glued to the *Englisch* vehicle as it pulled away from his home. Morning light was splashing across his fields, but what difference did it make? Leah was leaving. Leah was on her way to the hospital in Lewistown.

"I'm surprised they let Annie ride in the back," Adam said as Belinda joined their group.

"*Ya*, at first they didn't seem to believe she was a nurse." David laughed. The sound seemed foreign, out of place after Adam's long night. "When she pulled out her old hospital ID, the taller fellow nearly popped a lens off his glasses."

"It's not completely out of the ordinary for a family member to ride in the back of the ambulance," Belinda said.

She was short like Adam's mother, extremely thin and probably had seen the far side of sixty. He'd known her for several years. He and Leah had visited with her several times, but still Adam felt slightly uncomfortable around her—maybe because of her short, uncovered gray hair.

Or maybe his discomfort came from realizing Belinda was responsible for birthing so many of the Amish babies in their community. As she was the area midwife, they depended on her expertise, but she wasn't Amish. She existed in a gray area, somewhere in-between. Once he'd asked Annie why Belinda worked exclusively with Amish families. Annie had said Belinda considered it her ministry, but she wouldn't give any details of the woman's background. Adam's mother had shrugged and said, "She assisted with your birth, Adam. What more do you need to know?"

Belinda's words brought him back to the present.

"She kept Leah calm and was a help to the paramedics. She knew how to stay out of the way, and her nursing background could come in handy should Leah go into labor again."

"Is that a possibility?" Adam asked.

"It's not likely. They already started administering fluids through her IV." Belinda patted his arm. "Don't worry, Adam."

"Remember, she has our phone," Samuel said.

Belinda buttoned her coat. The sun was adding warmth to the day, but the temperatures were probably in the low forties. "She'll call me if Leah's condition changes, and we'll be with them shortly."

Adam nodded, but he still felt as if he were walking around half-awake. Was this all a bad dream? Would it soon be over? "All right. I'll be ready to go as soon as I look after the animals and—"

"Consider it done," David said. "I'll also post a note on your barn door for your customers, telling them you'll be in touch about their engine repairs."

With a groan, Adam thought of the shelves of work waiting for him.

"It will keep." Samuel seemed able to read his mind. "Go with Belinda. I'll ride over to your parents' farm to update them on all that has happened."

"*Danki.*" The single word seemed inadequate, but what else was there to say?

He climbed into Belinda's little car, and stared out the window as they sped away. Soon his dirt lane turned to blacktop and blacktop turned to freeway. He'd never enjoyed riding in automobiles, even when he was on his *rumspringa*, though perhaps those months were when he first realized he had a knack for working on small engines.

Machines fascinated him—parts and how they operated as a whole, especially when they were taken care of properly. But automobiles? No. The pace of travelling in them had always been too fast, and the way the cars' windows shut out all of the smells and sounds seemed wrong. He missed those things. They grounded him when he went to other places like someone else's home or the schoolhouse or town.

This morning was different. This morning he wanted to urge Belinda to drive faster.

And the fact he couldn't hear the sounds of the small towns they passed, or smell the scents from the restaurants or farms, those things didn't seem to matter. All that mattered was catching up with the ambulance, finding his way to the hospital, and hearing what the doctor had to say.

They could finish with administering their medicines, and then he'd take his wife home. Less than six hours had passed since he found Leah on the floor of the bathroom, but he was more than ready for this trial to be over.

Annie hadn't stepped into a hospital since the day she rushed out of the front doors of Mercy, the day she'd received a call her father had been in a buggy accident. It was hard to fathom that three years had passed. The time had flown!

As she walked into Lewistown Hospital, keeping pace beside Leah's stretcher, the familiar sound of monitor beeps, soft-soled shoes on linoleum floors, and nurses talking to patients showered her like the snowflakes that had begun falling again outside.

One of the paramedics, Stanley, pushed Leah through the double doors at the end of the hall and a nurse stepped in front of Annie, blocking her way. A few years older than Annie, she had glossy black hair flowing past her shoulders, pinned back away from her face, and a no-nonsense attitude. "I'm sorry, Miss. Family has to wait outside, at least until we have her admitted."

"Oh. Yes, but you see, I'm a nurse."

To give her credit, Nurse Gabriella—Annie could read her nametag now—raised an eyebrow but didn't so much as question her or show any other indication of softening on the regulations. "I'm proud to hear it, dear. Our waiting room is back that way. Someone will be out to see you as soon as your—"

"*Schweschder.*" The word came out softly as tears stung her eyes for the first time since hearing Samuel mention Leah's name.

"As soon as your sister is settled."

Annie reversed directions and walked slowly back into the waiting room. Samuel's phone felt like a stone in her apron pocket. She could call him, but what would she say? Leah's condition had remained the same during the twenty-five-minute ride. She expected Adam and Belinda would arrive any time. Perhaps it would be best to wait.

The phone was for emergencies, and this wasn't one—at least not at the moment.

The clock on the wall mocked her, its hands moving so slowly she thought it might be broken. Another patient arrived—a man with his arm wrapped in an old shirt, blood soaking through the cotton. Stanley walked back outside, back to his ambulance. Annie sat in the plastic chair and waited.

During her time as a nurse, the one thing she hadn't done was spend much time in the visitor's room. If she had her—

"Oh my goodness!" Jumping up, she hurried toward the emergency room doors that led back into the parking area. The first set of doors swished open and the cold air did more than any mug of coffee to waken her. She never made it outside though, as Stanley was returning once again through the second set of doors. Older, medium height, with skin as dark as the night, his smile immediately put her worries to rest—the smile and the quilting bag he held up in his right hand.

"Did you forget something, Nurse Annie?"

"*Danki*, Stanley. I may need that since it looks as if I've been banished to the waiting room."

Stanley actually laughed. "No worries. You know the drill. Once they have Leah transferred to a bed and confirm she's stable, they'll allow family members back."

Annie pulled in a deep breath as she accepted the bag filled with her quilting supplies. "*Ya*, you're right. I do know that. It was the same where I worked in Philadelphia, but rules are easy to forget when it's your loved one behind the emergency room doors."

"Don't I know it. My wife was back there a year ago. I was none too happy about waiting on this side."

Studying him, Annie realized how drama worked on your emotions. Normally she was sensitive to other people, but when she was in the middle of her own emergency, she'd immediately forgotten that other people weren't there only to serve her. It was easy to overlook people she came in contact with—yet they had families, problems, and worries the same as she did. "How is your wife now?"

"Good. She has to watch her cholesterol, but the docs gave her a stent and fixed her right up."

"*Wunderbaar.*"

Stanley's radio squawked and he reached to turn it down. "Best get out there or my partner is going to come looking for me. I'll be praying for your sister."

"*Danki.*"

Annie carried her quilt bag over to the waiting area. There wasn't much she could do with it yet. She had managed to finish her sample square. She pulled it out and stared at it—Overall Sam. She'd chosen dark blue fabric for his pants, green for his shirt, and the traditional black for his hat. In a word, he was adorable.

Was one of the babes Leah carried a boy?

Would he one day work beside her brother Adam, tilling the land, even learning to take apart small mechanical engines?

Annie ran her fingers over the stitching, closed her eyes, and began to pray. She prayed for the doctors who were looking over Leah's charts, for the nurses who were checking her IV, running her vitals, and making her comfortable. She prayed for the babies within her womb—for the two of them though she didn't know if they were boys or girls. She prayed for Leah, that she could remain at peace. She prayed for Adam as well, and was in the midst of asking God to give her wisdom and strength when she heard voices.

"I believe she's asleep."

"*Nein.* She's prayed that way—with her eyes squeezed shut—since she was a *kind.*" Adam tumbled into the chair beside her.

Belinda sat across from her, wearing a smile, snow covering the top of her coat. "Been waiting out here long?"

"I'm not sure. I don't think so . . ." Annie glanced up at the clock on the wall, surprised to see twenty minutes had passed. "Less than half an hour. I tried to go back, but they wouldn't let me."

"Lewistown has strict rules. Some hospitals, not so much. Since several of my patients have been transferred here over the years, I might be able to find out something." Belinda stood and brushed at the snow on her coat, then strode past the information desk and through the double doors.

"I like her more all the time," Adam admitted.

"Is that so?"

"*Ya.* I expected her to yak, yak, yak all the way here, but for an *Englischer* she's remarkably quiet."

"Adam, that's a terrible stereotype."

"Would it have been better to say for a woman she's remarkably quiet?"

"*Nein.* You're tired, cranky, and worried."

"I am." He leaned forward in his chair, elbows on his knees, head resting on his hands. He'd taken the time to dress properly and had on clothes so similar to the sample square she was holding that Annie nearly started laughing. Overall Sam indeed. Overall Adam!

If all of this could end well, she'd rename the boy on the quilt.

Belinda pushed through the doors. "Leah has been admitted. The doctor is with her now and would like to see you, Adam."

Adam glanced up, a look of confusion coloring his features.

"Go, Adam." Annie prodded him with her foot.

"*Ya.* Of course." He stood, but didn't move.

"Through the doors," Belinda said. "I'll show you the way."

Adam glanced back at her, and Annie felt something in her heart twist. She wanted to go with him, wanted to take his hand and follow him back into Leah's room.

But this moment was between Adam and Leah and the doctors. There would be enough time for her to help later. For now, she would stay in the waiting room, holding the material for the quilt she had yet to make, and praying for Leah and her unborn children.

11

The hospital gown felt foreign against Leah's skin and skimpy—especially the back portion where there was a distinct draft! She was relieved when the nurse helped her into the bed and pulled the covers up over her. At least they'd allowed her to keep her prayer *kapp* on. Annie had helped her fasten it over her long blonde hair before the paramedics had arrived at their home. The braid and bun were a mess, but her head was covered. There would be time to re-comb it all later.

Worrying about such a thing might seem trivial to some people, but Leah had never been out in public with her hair uncovered. She had enough to think about right now without feeling self-conscious about her hair. It wasn't so much that she feared it would be a sin. She was certain God would understand.

No, it was more a feeling she'd left much of her old life behind when she'd been lifted into the ambulance. The prayer covering was a small symbol of who she was and all she had embraced when she joined the church—it helped her retain her balance and identity. Silly, maybe, but at this moment she needed to keep as much of her old life as possible with her.

Nurse Gabriella was adjusting the second bag of IV fluid—the one with the medicine—and practically clucking like a mother hen when Adam walked in with the doctor.

"How are you feeling?" Worry marked Adam's face like age lines on the old men who sat around watching the *kinner* play baseball. She marveled how the last twenty-four hours had brought them together, almost as close as when they were first married.

"Hot and a little nauseous."

"The pains—"

"They've stopped, Adam. The medicines they're giving to me, they are working very well."

"That's *gut*, then. We did the right thing to come." He waited next to her bed, his hand touching her shoulder, and Leah was suddenly sure they'd done the right thing. She'd never been inside an *Englisch* hospital before, but it wasn't so frightening with Adam standing by her side.

Doctor Kentlee had walked in with Adam, and he stood now at the end of her bed, studying her chart. It wasn't written on paper the way Samuel kept records. Instead, her information seemed to be kept on some sort of computer board. There was no doubt it was her chart though, for his gaze moved from the monitors, to her, then back to the tablet.

Handing it to Nurse Gabriella, he looked directly at Leah. "The magnesium we are giving you is what stopped the contractions."

"*Ya.* The nurse explained it to me. It makes me a little sick, but that is better than the pains."

"Magnesium can also cause you to be flushed and even tired." He was older and had no hair on top of his head. The light from the morning sun shone through the windows lining one side of the room. The sun's rays made the top of his head somewhat shiny. It was difficult to be afraid of a man with a polished head. Plus, he had very kind blue eyes, covered by white bushy eyebrows and wrinkles spreading out from the sides.

"It will be *gut* to rest," Leah agreed. "It was a long night."

"I imagine it was." Dr. Kentlee pointed to the fetal monitor she was wearing. "We'll run the magnesium for forty-eight hours, and we'll need to leave the monitor on while we do."

Leah touched the blanket, which covered her gown, where it pooched out from the stretchy band and monitor placed around her stomach.

"Can't say I ever wore a belt before," she admitted, rubbing her stomach. "It will feel *gut* to take it off."

"The monitor allows us to measure your babies' heart rates continuously." Dr. Kentlee held up what looked a little like Samuel's stethoscope. "I'll admit to being somewhat old-fashioned though. I still like to listen myself. Do you mind?"

Leah glanced at Adam, and they both shook their head no. They didn't mind at all. This doctor had helped their babies, and what he'd instructed the paramedics to do had helped them.

Maybe he had saved their lives.

She moved her arm, the one with the IV in it, on top of the metal handrail.

"Belinda has one of those," Leah said.

"A doppler?"

"*Ya.*"

"Belinda would be your midwife then."

Leah nodded as Gabriella pulled down the blanket. Dr. Kentlee placed his doppler on the mound that was her stomach. Leah was used to this process—Belinda, Samuel, and even Annie had listened to the babies' heartbeats before. They'd even encouraged her to listen, though mostly all she had heard was a swish-swish sound that reminded her of swimming in the creek.

Dr. Kentlee's eyes went up and around and finally met hers. When they did, he smiled nicely and more of the tension in Leah's shoulders melted away. She glanced up at Adam, but Adam was frowning at the doppler. He'd never cared much for medical procedures. Once he had admitted to her that he didn't understand how Annie would choose such a thing to spend her *rumspringa* on—most of the things his sister did when helping patients made him nauseous.

"All right." Dr. Kentlee pulled the instrument off his ears and settled onto the chair beside her bed.

Gabriella pulled up the blanket and tucked it around Leah, as if she were cold. She wasn't cold, but it did help her feel more—well, more covered and she was grateful for that. She smiled her thanks.

"The heartbeats for both babies sound strong, but we're not out of the woods *yet*." His emphasis on the word *yet* set off warning bells.

"You mean the *bopplin* are still in danger?"

"Hard to say, Adam."

Leah was surprised the doctor knew her husband's name, but then they had walked in together. Perhaps they'd introduced themselves in the hall.

"But you're the doctor."

"A doctor, yes. A prophet, no." The white eyebrows wiggled. "Leah experienced preterm labor—something fairly common with twins. It has slowed with her first few doses of magnesium sulfate, which I'd like to continue for at least forty-eight hours."

"Two days isn't so bad," Adam muttered.

Leah knew he was worried about their being away from the farm. She didn't like it either.

"I'm concerned there may be other things going on we're not seeing here. Perhaps the early contractions were a warning sign. I'd like to run a few tests."

"Why?" Adam asked, becoming more agitated.

Dr. Kentlee didn't answer immediately. Instead he waited for quietness to settle around them. Then he asked Adam a question. "Do you work in the fields?"

"*Ya.* Some. I have a small place."

"That's good. Your children will be able to learn the old ways."

Adam nodded.

Leah wondered how much this *Englisch* doctor knew about their way of life. No doubt, he did see many Amish patients at this hospital.

"And what do you grow?"

"Corn and hay."

When the doctor only waited, Adam added, "The hay is a mixture of clover, alsike, alfalfa, and timothy."

Dr. Kentlee grunted. "Good blend. If you noticed your corn, or your hay, was not producing as it should you wouldn't immediately run out and apply more fertilizer . . ."

Adam didn't speak, only shook his head.

"You'd check it out. Try to find out what was wrong."

"Are you comparing me to hay?" Leah asked, her fear draining away as she tried to decide if she was offended.

"Hay is a blessing from the Lord, *fraa.*"

"I was using the farming metaphor so Adam would understand why we need to do a few tests." Kentlee stood and patted her hand. "I'll be back before your evening meal. We should know more by then."

<hr />

Adam had experienced slow afternoons before.

The day his father was in the hospital had stretched on end-lessly, one wretched hour dragging past the next. He'd stayed home to look after the farm, and no one had a telephone then. So he'd waited for the bishop to hear from the *Englischer* who lived across the street, and then he drove his buggy out to tell him how things had gone. It had been a long day.

Then there had been the afternoon before his marriage to Leah. It had seemed to scuff along like an old workhorse, tak-ing much longer to pass than was possible.

But this afternoon? He wasn't the type of person to watch a clock, but the one on the wall in Leah's room did nothing but frustrate him. Every time he glanced at it, the hands had barely crept another ten minutes forward.

At least the nurses had allowed Annie to join them in the room.

"Why aren't you quilting?" Adam nodded toward the bag he'd seen her carry from the waiting room to Leah's room. "Not enough material?"

Annie sighed. "Oh, I have plenty of fabric. I purchased the last of it when I was in town with Leah on Saturday."

"Then why are you crocheting?"

Tugging on the ball of yarn one more time, Annie smiled. "Things often don't work as we plan. Right? I put all my quilt-ing supplies into my bag. Everything is measured and ready, but I neglected to wash and iron the fabric first."

"Why would you need to wash new fabric?"

"There are several reasons—"

"It's not dirty though. It's *new*."

"*Ya*, but sometimes with new fabric the colors will bleed. It's best to wash them separately, before you sew them together."

"Sounds like a lot of trouble for a blanket."

"Oh, Adam. A quilt is much more than a blanket."

"If you say so."

Annie gave him a you-should-know-better look and continued working with the crochet needle and yellow yarn. She'd purchased both from the gift shop an hour ago. It looked to Adam like she was making a blanket, and probably a baby blanket at that, but then he didn't know much about the wonders women did with yarn—only that one needle meant crocheting and two meant knitting.

Given the color—a soft yellow—Leah could assume Annie was making something for the babies they were waiting on, but playing it safe as far as a boy or a girl. The thought brought a smile to his face just as an orderly rolled Leah back into the room.

"All done with the test?" he asked.

"Ya. It was no problem." She went on to describe the sonogram procedure to him, but it was beyond anything he could imagine. Amish families generally did not have pictures made of their babies, before or after they were born.

Belinda had suggested having one done when they'd first learned of the twins, but they had both declined. Since Leah seemed healthy it hadn't been medically necessary, but now—well, now it apparently was.

"Is she back in her room for good?" he asked Gabriella.

"We're all done," she assured him. "My shift ends at three, but I'll be in to check on you one more time before I go."

Soon Leah was napping. He didn't understand how she could sleep with that needle in her arm. The sight of it made him a little queasy. He'd finally given in and eaten the part of her lunch she didn't want, but now he thought the half of club sandwich and tomato soup might be headed back up if he stared at the needle and long tube snaking into it much longer.

"Look away, Adam."

"What?"

"I've seen that look on your face before. Remember the time you had to help me at the schoolhouse? I was giving flu shots and I needed someone to hold the children."

"Don't remind me." Adam put his head between his knees, the way he'd done that day. Most of the children hadn't minded the needle Annie had stuck into their shoulders, but Adam had gone outside and thrown up in the outhouse. He didn't mind a shot when he had to have one—Samuel had given him one last year for tetanus. Watching while he did it though? That was not something he could do. Sharp objects shouldn't go into your arm, and plastic tubes shouldn't snake out. They certainly shouldn't stay there like the one in Leah's arm.

Better to think about the engines in his shop. Engines were made of metal. They didn't pierce easily, and they didn't bleed if you dropped them on the ground.

How was he going to be a father?

Infants were extremely small and helpless.

Who was he fooling? He'd probably faint away the first time he held one of the babies.

"Breathe deeper. You're starting to look green."

"How can you tell that? I have my head practically between my knees."

"I'm a nurse. Remember? I'm trained to know the signs of someone who is about to hurl." Annie put aside her crochet work, stood, and brought him a glass of ice water. "Drink this. It will help."

"I doubt it."

"Do what I say, *bruder*. This one time."

Adam downed the small Styrofoam cup of water in one gulp. He did feel better. Standing, he walked around the room. It was too small to pace in, but at least he could look out the window. Seeing the half-inch of snow in the parking lot, covering the trees, helped to ease some of his anxiety. Nature marched on regardless of what was upsetting his little world.

"Where did Belinda go?"

"She had an appointment to check on one of her mothers-to-be."

"Do you still have Samuel's phone? In case we need to call her? We might need a ride home. It's possible they could release her early if—"

Annie put a hand on his arm. "Try not to worry. I sent the phone with Belinda. She's going to give it back to Samuel. He might need it."

"But—"

"We have the phone on Leah's nightstand. It's free to use. We can call Belinda or even Samuel."

"*Ya.* That's right. I forgot about that one."

Annie sat back down and resumed her crocheting.

Leah continued napping.

And Adam went back to worrying. "Do you think we'll be able to go home tonight?"

"*Nein.* They'll want to give her the magnesium through tomorrow. It's possible—"

He never heard the rest of her sentence, because the door to Leah's room opened. Dr. Kentlee walked in and Adam knew, positively knew by the look on his face they were not going home. In fact, he had the sickening feeling what the doctor was about to say was much, much worse.

12

Annie pushed the crochet needle into her yarn and the yarn into her quilting bag. Leah had begun to stir as soon as Dr. Kentlee walked into the room. It was nice to see Gabriella trail in behind him. The clock on the wall said ten minutes after three. Either Gabriella's replacement was late, which was doubtful, or she was staying around to complete final rounds with Dr. Kentlee.

Annie made eye contact with the woman and nodded her thanks.

"I can't believe I fell asleep." Leah's expression turned sheepish as she accepted a cup of water from the nurse.

"Your body's adjusting to a lot of things," Annie said. "Sleep is one way of coping."

"Leah and Adam, I'd like to talk to you about your test results." Dr. Kentlee's expression appeared very grave. He continued staring at the screen on the tablet, apparently scrolling through reports. Finally, he handed it back to Gabriella. "I assume you want Annie to stay in the room while I go over this?"

"*Ya*. We do." Adam had been standing near the window, but he moved closer to her and Leah, not stopping until he was standing shoulder-to-shoulder with Annie, who was right next to Leah's bed. Everything about Adam's posture and their position together seemed to scream red alert, as if together they would be able to confront whatever was coming next and draw strength from one another.

Annie prayed they could.

"I'm not going to sugarcoat this. The ultrasound indicates the babies aren't as developed as we thought."

"You said their heartbeat was *gut*." Adam ran his fingers over and through his curly hair, sending it into complete disarray.

Dr. Kentlee held up his hand, palm out. "Yes, and that hasn't changed. However, since this is your first sonogram, Belinda was guessing at your exact date of conception. You thought you were into your thirty-sixth week. The sonogram you had a few hours ago suggests the babies may be younger."

"How much younger?" Annie asked. She understood where the doctor was headed now, and why he was worried. She also knew that Adam and Leah were lost as to why this was so important.

"Ten days, certainly a little more than a week."

"So what does this mean?" Leah spoke up as she placed a protective hand over her stomach. "That the babies aren't actually due at the end of December? Instead they're due the first week in January?"

"Yes . . ." Dr. Kentlee drew out the word. "But, Leah, you're not going to make it until January. My goal, our goal, will be for you to make it until December, another two weeks. If you can wait to deliver until then, the chances of complications will be much less."

"Complications?" Adam's voice hardened. "What types of complications?"

"Low birth rate is tied to many things. We don't have to go into those now—"

"Tell us. We need to know, if we're to make informed decisions." Adam gripped the side rail of the bed with both hands.

Annie glanced down and saw that his knuckles were white, his grasp on the rail was so fierce.

"Leah and I are adults," Adam continued. "We are parents to these children, even though they aren't born yet. Now what are these complications?"

The doctor didn't avoid the question. Instead he moved his gaze from Adam to Leah and then back again. "Infants with low birth weight have an increased risk for a wide variety of problems—everything from mental retardation to cerebral palsy. There can also be vision or hearing loss. This doesn't mean your babies would have these problems if they were born early. Only that they could."

"What about their lungs?" Annie asked.

"Should be fine. Up to thirty-four weeks, we administer a steroid called betamethazone to help develop the babies' lungs more quickly."

"But the contractions have stopped," Leah protested.

"And that's a good sign. Also, you're definitely past thirty-four weeks, so the steroid isn't necessary. Our problem is that your babies are very small." Dr. Kentlee handed the tablet to Gabriella and pushed his hands into the pockets of his lab coat. "What I'm going to suggest will be very difficult for you, I suspect. I've worked with other Amish families over the years, and I understand your ties to your family and your home. In my opinion, Leah needs to be under close observation for the rest of this week and all of next—until the babies pass the thirty-six-week mark."

"You want her to stay here?" Adam's voice rose in disbelief. "In Lewistown? For two weeks?"

"No. No, I don't. We don't have the facilities here, don't have a neonatal unit. I'd like to transfer her to a hospital that does."

Annie closed her eyes. Some part of her had known this might be coming. When they'd first stepped into the corridor of the Lewistown Hospital, she'd known this might be the first of several stops.

"Another hospital?" Adam turned and began pacing back and forth across the five feet in front of the window. "What other hospital? Where?"

"There are several good facilities in Philadelphia."

Adam sank into the chair, speechless, his mouth half open.

The room grew so quiet that the sound of the clock ticking increased until Annie thought it would surely plop off the wall. Then she remembered her time working at Mercy, her time of *rumspringa*.

"Adam, Mercy Hospital has a neonatal unit."

He stared at her as if she'd spoken in French.

"It's true," Dr. Kentlee said. "We've transferred to Mercy before."

"I was on staff there for a while," Annie explained. She turned to Leah. "It's a *gut* place. They are one of the top medical facilities in the state with kind people, and it's a quiet, gentle setting."

Leah glanced around the room. Adam was now sitting with his head between his hands as if he were suffering from a throbbing headache.

"I have to go to the bathroom," Leah said abruptly, as if the conversation going on around her was not where she'd be spending the next two weeks and where her children would most likely be born.

"Oh, all right." Annie lowered the safety rail on the side of the bed.

"Let me help you." Gabriella moved to adjust the pole holding the two IV bags.

Together they assisted Leah, being sure she was steady on her feet, before helping her shuffle over to the small bathroom.

What happened next happened so quickly that even Annie would later have trouble telling Samuel about it when she called him on the hospital room phone.

It seemed Leah cried out, with a sound like a small animal caught in a trap. She tried to collapse to the floor, but Gabriella and Annie were both there on either side of her, and they had her by the arms before she could do more than sink an inch or so.

The blood spreading down her legs and onto the floor was substantial, and when Adam saw it he turned white and fainted dead away. Dr. Kentlee strode to the wall and hit the emergency button, calling for help. Then he was at their side. Together they picked Leah up and placed her back on the bed.

By that time, she, too, had lost consciousness.

―――∞――――

Leah woke in a different room.

She opened her eyes and fought through the fog to remember all that had happened. More than anything, she wanted to raise her hand, caress her stomach—her babies, but her hand was so heavy she couldn't. So, instead she focused on Annie, who was sitting a few feet away.

In her lap she held the white fabric they'd picked out together, and she seemed to be working on one of the appliqués for the baby quilt. She turned the fabric toward the window, where the blinds were partially open to allow a patch of light through. Leah could make out the dark and light blue fabric Annie had chosen to use in one of the Sunbonnet Sue dresses.

Tears stung her eyes and began to roll down her cheeks.

Surely her babies were okay. Annie wouldn't be making the quilt if . . . if anything had happened.

Sensing Leah was awake, Annie raised her eyes. She didn't move immediately. Instead a slow, full smile replaced the look of concentration. She glanced down, worked her sewing needle into the edge of her quilt block, and placed the fabric in her quilting bag. Standing, she adjusted the blinds to allow even more light into the room, then walked to the side of the bed and poured a cup of water from the pitcher on the bedside table.

"It's *gut* to see your eyes open." She used the control pad to raise the head of the bed. "Try to drink a little. I imagine your mouth feels as if you've been swallowing cotton."

Leah nodded. She managed to lift her hand to help with the cup, but her arm felt weak and unsteady. She noticed the IV was still in, though this time it was in her opposite arm. With both hands, she gingerly touched her stomach. The babies weren't moving, but her abdomen was as large as ever and that was a comfort.

"The *bopplin* are *gut*. You can see their heartbeats on this monitor." Annie pointed to a digital display where two lines marched constantly from left to right. A number showed brightly above each line.

"The number—it's what it should be?"

"*Ya.*"

Annie offered her another drink and this time she finished what was in the cup.

Leah stared around the room, trying to piece together the fragments of what she remembered and separate it from her dreams.

There were now two chairs in her room—the one Annie had been quilting in and one closer to her bed. Annie sat in it and waited.

"I don't remember a lot." Leah's voice was scratchy, like the time she'd had a cold for a week and missed school. "We were talking with the older Doctor . . ."

"Dr. Kentlee."

"And I had to . . ." she glanced around the room, her gaze finally landing on the bathroom door, which was now to the left of the door leading out to the hall. "I had to use the toilet, something terrible."

Annie nodded, but didn't interrupt.

"I think." Leah could feel her heart beating faster. Had it been a dream, or had it happened? "I think I remember a lot of blood and maybe you praying over me. Or did I dream that?"

Reaching for her hand, Annie laced their fingers together. "You didn't dream it."

"And then I don't remember very much clearly . . . faces—some I didn't know, and some I did." She stared down at their hands. "But the *bopplin* are all right?"

"Yes. Now they are."

"Why did they place me in a different room?"

The surprise showed on Annie's face. "We're not at Lewistown anymore. You began bleeding because your placenta separated partially from your uterine lining. When that happened, the doctors at Lewistown stabilized you, gave you a blood transfusion, and then transferred you here to Mercy."

"In Philadelphia?"

"*Ya.* An ambulance brought you, and I rode along. Adam, he rode with Belinda."

"Adam was here?"

"For a while."

Leah fingered the white bed covering, digesting all that Annie had said. She'd had a blood transfusion? She'd ridden in an ambulance? Again?

"Why can't I remember any of this?"

"You slept through much of it. And sometimes, when you've been through a traumatic experience, your mind chooses not to remember. It could be bits and pieces will come back later."

Leah nodded as if she understood, but she didn't. None of what Annie had said made any sense at all.

She closed her eyes and began to pray. Thanking God her babies had strong hearts. That whatever had happened, had happened while she was in the hospital. And that Annie was there to explain things to her. She liked receiving information slowly, so she could process it, think about it, and pray about it. She didn't consider herself stupid, but everything had happened so fast. She needed time to digest all of these changes.

Annie must have thought she'd fallen asleep. She patted her hand, placed it under the blanket, and stood to move back to her quilting.

"Explain to me about the placenta again."

"It's what provides oxygen and nutrients to your *bopplin*."

"But it tore?"

"Yes. Not completely, or you would have gone into labor."

"There was a lot of blood." Leah didn't open her eyes.

"Yes."

"It was my blood though—not the babies'."

"Correct."

Leah opened her eyes. "I don't mind losing my blood."

"I know you don't, but we have to keep you strong, and we have to keep the placenta attached as long as possible."

Nodding, Leah tried to absorb all that Annie was saying. "When did Adam go home?"

"Wednesday night, when the doctors said all three of you were out of danger."

Leah stared out the window. For the first time, she noticed that beyond the blinds were many buildings—an entire city she hadn't even realized surrounded her.

"He calls every night. He goes to our house and uses Samuel's phone."

Tears threatened to spill again, but Leah blinked them back. It was time to be strong, for both her husband and her children. Her mind and heart were flooded with memories of Adam holding her on their bathroom floor, his arms around her, his heartbeat against her skin. She knew how much he cared for her, and she wouldn't doubt him again.

"So I'll stay here until it's time?"

"Yes. The doctors—you have two—hope to postpone the birth two more weeks, until at least December 7th."

Leah closed her eyes. Two more weeks? Without Adam? Here in the middle of Philadelphia? She wanted to shout or cry or throw something.

Instead, she pulled in two deep, steadying breaths. When she opened her eyes, Annie was studying her, waiting.

"We're both going to need something to help us pass the hours. It's a *gut* thing you brought that quilt. The fabric isn't as stiff, as if it's been washed."

"My landlady did that for me."

"Landlady?" Perhaps this was all a dream. Maybe she'd wake up in a little while and be back on the bathroom floor, Adam behind her, waiting for Annie and Samuel to arrive.

Annie retrieved the quilting bag and settled in the chair next to the bed, adjusting the blinds again so even more light spilled across the floor. Leah noticed more details now, like the cozy feel of the room. The walls were a warm rose color, and there were two shelves across from her bed—she supposed for flowers. *Englischers* were big on purchasing what grew freely in the fields. This was something she and Adam had laughed over when they'd passed the small florist in town. Since there were no flowers on her shelves, someone had placed a small ceramic jar painted blue with yellow daisies. It brightened up the place and helped Leah think of summer.

Above the second shelf hung a small decorative cross. It was wooden, simple, and seemed to be made of maple. Whoever made it had shellacked it so that the grains of the wood shone. Leah couldn't help thinking of Annie's *Onkel* Eli—he would appreciate the workmanship by whoever had made the symbol of their faith. Though Amish didn't normally decorate with crosses, somehow this one brought her a sense of peace.

"Family aren't allowed to spend the night," Annie was explaining. "It was Samuel's idea for me to contact my old landlady, the one I lived with when I was working here. She happened to have a room open—a small one with two twin beds, so I took it."

"And you're walking back and forth?" Leah glanced out the window. Though the sun was shining, it was nearly Thanksgiving. Surely the temperature was cold.

"It isn't far—a few blocks. I walked when I lived here before. Actually I enjoy the stroll."

Leah watched her as Annie ran her fingers around the Sunbonnet Sue dress. "So your landlady washed and ironed the fabric? I know you and your quilting ways. You always do both first."

Annie nodded in agreement. "Yes, she did. Vickie asked if there was anything she could do for you, and I admitted I'd like to be working on your quilt—"

"Sounds like quite the landlady."

"Indeed she is."

But there was no more quilting that morning. One of the nurses came in—and yes, it brought a smile to Leah's face to see her. She wore the same long conservative dress and the same nurse's cap that Annie had worn that first evening so long ago, when she'd come home to care for Jacob.

126

She peeked at Annie, and knew that she was remembering the same thing. Then they were both grinning.

As the nurse went about charting Leah's status and performing her various duties, Annie explained what they found so amusing. After all, Samuel's confusion over Annie's clothing had been the beginning of their relationship—a relationship which resulted in their marriage and the child she was carrying.

"I remember hearing about you," Nurse Penny admitted. She was taller than Annie and bigger—not in a soft way, but strong. Leah had no doubt she could handle whatever needed doing. Her skin was very white with freckles across the bridge of her nose, and her hair was short and bright red. "Mercy Hospital was famous for a while when Annie worked here. We became quite the talk because we had an Amish nurse."

"We still have one," Leah piped up.

"I suppose you do." Penny cocked her head. "I've been nursing ten years, and if I walked away from my job today, I'd still be a nurse, now wouldn't I?"

Leah and Annie both nodded.

"But I won't be walking away, Miss Leah. We're going to see these babies through to the day of their birth when you and your husband will hold them in your arms." She adjusted the bed so that Leah was more comfortable. "Now I'll send someone to help you with your shower in about an hour. You rest up until then."

After she'd left the room, Leah turned to Annie. "You were right—this is the best place for me to be."

"*Ya*. They're *gut* here. You can see why I accepted a job when they offered one. I felt comfortable working with the staff. It's as if they've kept some of the old ways, with their manner of dress and the simple furnishings—"

"Also, the way they treat people."

"Yes. That, too. But they have the newest technology, medically speaking. I'm glad Dr. Kentlee agreed to transfer you to Mercy."

Leah studied her sister-in-law. "Do you ever miss it? You spent a lot of time studying, working to earn your nursing certification. I know how much it means to you to be able to help others."

"I still help others as *Gotte* sees fit."

"True . . ."

"I don't miss the city." Annie turned and stared out the window. "It always crowded in around me. I endured it so I could learn the things I wanted to know. The hospital—this place was like a sanctuary, and I'll admit I do miss it at times. I miss the people and the children, of course."

Leah nodded.

"But I no longer question my decision. *Gotte* asks us to make sacrifices at different times in our life. Mine was small. To give up a job so that I can work alongside Samuel and help those in our community and have a family of my own? I surrendered one dream for something better than I could have ever imagined."

13

Leah didn't actually start quilting that afternoon. She rested, had her shower, and ate her lunch. She was surprised to find she did have an appetite.

When the doctors came in, she actually understood what they said, thanks to the fact that Annie had already explained so much of what was happening.

The first surprise was Dr. Reese, who was tall, thin, and beautiful. She had dark black hair cut shoulder length and her eyes were a dark brown that seemed to catch everything.

"I'll deliver your babies, Leah." Dr. Reese didn't bother sitting. She seemed to have a lot of energy, as if even standing still in one place was hard for her.

"You've delivered twins before?"

Dr. Reese shared a smile with Annie.

"A few."

"Dr. Reese specializes in multiple births," Annie explained.

"Oh." Leah glanced from her new doctor to her sister-in-law. "Twins and triplets."

"We have our share of quads here as well. Higher than that is rare." Dr. Reese went on to explain that the babies' weight should steadily increase over the next two weeks. She knew the sex and asked if Leah wanted to know.

"*Nein.* I don't think so. At least not until I speak with my husband."

"That's fine." Dr. Reese smiled. "Many couples would rather be surprised. I'll be in to check on you each day, and the nurses will page me should anything unusual pop up."

The babies also had their own doctor.

He couldn't have been more different from Dr. Reese. Shorter, he was built rather like one of David's bulls. His skin was as dark as night, but when he smiled, which he did as soon as Leah glanced up, it lit his entire face. His hair was a fuzzy white, and his hands were quite large.

"How are my babies?" he asked.

She'd expected his voice to be booming, but it wasn't. In fact, when he spoke it reminded her of molasses pouring over pancakes.

"Leah, this is Doctor Kamal. He's a neonatal specialist."

Kamal took her hand in his, and she was surprised that it was as soft as his voice. "She means I work with the very small ones."

Dr. Kamal had an unusual accent, rising and falling like the song of one of the night birds she would sometimes listen to as she sat out in the rocker on the porch back home.

"These small ones, they are precious, yes?"

Leah nodded.

"So we handle them with special care. We try to wait, which is why you are here, under the care of the esteemed Dr. Reese." Again the smile, revealing the row of perfect white teeth.

"When they are ready though . . ." Kamal glanced at the cross, then at Annie, and finally at Leah. He moved down the bed, waiting for her to nod her permission. Annie pulled down the cover and sheet. He put both of his hands on her, and she was surprised to see that together they completely covered her huge stomach. "When they are ready, we will work together and bring them into this world—you and I, with the help of the Maker who knows all things."

He closed his eyes for a moment. Leah wasn't surprised at all when the babies moved, ever so slightly. Who wouldn't respond to such kindness? Dr. Kamal smiled, then pulled up the blankets.

"What questions do you have for me?"

She did have questions, and was relieved to find that she felt comfortable enough with the good doctor to ask them. So they talked for another ten minutes.

When he left, she lay back and closed her eyes, and Annie resumed her quilting. She hadn't made much progress since Leah had first awakened that morning. Peeking through one eye, Leah saw her pull out the Sunbonnet Sue, pink fabric on top of rose.

Leah closed her eyes, but occasionally she'd steal a glance and watch Annie as she stitched around the Dutch doll—or was it Amish? In her mind it had always been Amish, though the tourists who bought the finished quilts in the shops often referred to them as the Dutch doll quilts.

Soon the nurse would be back to take care of her afternoon monitoring, and then it would be time for dinner. She was glad the day had passed quickly. She was anxious to speak with Adam.

But for now it felt good to sit in what remained of the afternoon sun and watch Annie sew.

"Tell me a story."

"Say again." Annie's needle paused in mid-stitch.

"You've read dozens, probably hundreds, of books. I can't possibly sleep anymore. Tell me a story."

Annie dropped the quilt square in her lap, traced the black bonnet with her finger, and glanced sideways at Leah.

"What are you thinking of?"

"A story I'm not sure you'll want to hear."

"Oh, I want to hear it. I can tell by the way your eyebrows went up then down." Leah struggled to sit up straighter. "Go on. You can keep sewing while you talk."

Annie laughed, and the sound did more to confirm to Leah's heart all would be fine than the assurances of a dozen doctors.

"I was thinking about when I first came here to Mercy Hospital, about the first time I started an IV on a small child."

Leah stared down at the line snaking into her arm.

Annie waited for Leah to meet her gaze and nod, then she resumed her sewing and her voice took on the tone of a story-teller. Leah had heard her before, after Sunday church with the children in the barn or by the creek. She let Annie's words flow over her—allowed the images to seep into her heart.

<hr>

Bethany was not quite four years old. She came in presenting with a high fever and listlessness and I was working in the emergency room that morning, though it wasn't my regular rotation. I'd been asked to fill in for a nurse who was out sick. The child could barely raise her head. I'd been around sick children before—back home I'd taken care of Adam, Charity, and Reba when they were ill, but I'd never seen anything close to Bethany.

Her eyes were hollow, sunken actually, and her cheeks sported two bright red spots.

The mother was beside herself. I don't even remember her name now. Bethany, though, is one child I'll remember if I live to be ninety. She couldn't lift her arm, didn't even flinch when I had to stick her twice to start the IV, but she raised her brown eyes and stared into mine and I thought . . . I thought I'd been caressed by something very special.

We never did hear her cry. When she started receiving fluids, she did sleep a little. The fever raged on and on. They transferred her upstairs to pediatrics, which was my floor, so I was able to continue to see her. I would go in after my shift and wipe her down with cool rags. They'd instantly warm when they touched her skin, and always her brown eyes would stare into mine.

This went on for three days. I heard the other nurses talking about how hopeless it was, how the doctors had determined it was some bacterial infection and the antibiotics weren't working. I saw the father twice. He was a broken hulk of a man who would walk into the room, stare at his daughter, and then creep back to the hall. The mother though? She was like a tall tree standing in the forest. As if the fire was raging around her, but she refused to give in to it.

On the fourth day, I checked in early for my shift. Shelly, our supervisor, warned me that Bethany wasn't expected to make it through the day. I went into her room, and Bethany's mother was there beside her bed, kneeling on the cold linoleum and praying. It must have been a trick of the morning light, something to do with the blinds, but it seemed there was a ray of sunshine coming in and shining on Bethany, shining on the mother.

Bethany was sitting up in the bed and had one hand touching her mother's head. With the other hand she was sucking on her two fingers. It was the first time I saw her smile. Two days later she went home with her parents.

They never decided—conclusively—what was wrong with her.

Some of the things I read in the papers, they are terrible indeed. Even situations I see within our community, when I go on calls with Belinda or Samuel—it's not always pleasant or right or good. But when my heart is hurting, when I wake in the middle of the night and have trouble wondering why this world is as it is, my mind *always returns to that morning. I remember the image of the mother, kneeling by her child's bed and the child with her hand blessing her mother and the light coming through the dirt-smeared window.*

I wonder what healed the child.

Perhaps it had been the medicine.

Maybe the mother's love for Bethany had saved her.

Possibly Bethany's love for her parents had strengthened her.

Annie snipped the thread and held up the pink and rose Sunbonnet Sue. "What do you think?"

"That's it? What do I think of your quilting?"

Annie turned it back toward her with a frown. "Did I do something wrong?"

"With the quilting, *nein*. With the storytelling, possibly."

"Because?"

"Because I'd have more of her story, please. You always were a tease, Annie. Always leaving your listeners wanting more."

"Stories are that way though. They involve you in another's life, but our road only intersects theirs for a time."

"And you didn't see Bethany again?"

"I didn't." Annie helped Leah sit forward, plumped the pillows behind her, and rubbed the muscles in her neck and along her back.

She hadn't realized those muscles were stiff from sitting in the bed until Annie began massaging them. Was that another thing she learned in nursing school? Wherever she'd learned it, Leah offered up a prayer of thanksgiving she had. Perhaps she'd take another lap around the hospital corridor after her dinner came. Though it was cumbersome dragging along the IV pole, she'd found time out of the bed raised her spirits and helped the aches and pains brought on from too much sitting.

Annie would need to go before darkness fell outside. She was about to ask if they had time to attempt a stroll, which reminded her she needed to thank her sister-in-law for all she was doing, when the phone rang for the first time that day. They both knew who it was.

Annie once more adjusted the pillows, resettled Leah back against the bed, and then reached for the receiver.

14

Adam stood in Samuel's barn, gripping the cell phone so tightly he feared he might break it. The phone on the other end, the phone in Leah's hospital room, rang once, twice, and a third time. When he was sure no one would answer it, someone picked up the receiver. Then there was a shuffling sound as if one person were passing it to another.

Finally, his wife's voice travelled over the line.

"Hello?"

"Leah? Oh, Leah. I can't believe it's you."

"Did you call the wrong number?" she teased, and then he knew it was Leah and she was better, much better than she'd been in a long time.

"Maybe I did. Maybe I called the past. It sounds as if my *fraa* from a year ago is speaking with me."

There was silence on the line, and he wondered if he'd said something wrong. He'd been in the habit of doing so. Perhaps he'd done it again.

"I rather feel like my old self again, Adam, except for my stomach. It's still as big as ever."

"*Gut.*" He closed his eyes, breathed a prayer of such gratitude his heart actually hurt, and sat back on the wooden crate outside Samuel's horse stalls. "I called last night, but Annie answered. Tonight I hoped and prayed it would be you—"

His words fell away.

How could he explain the way each day had dragged on as he worked in the barn at their home, as he worked on the engines and with the animals? How could he describe how empty their house was without her there?

"I woke up this morning and thought I was still in Lewistown," she admitted.

Adam switched the phone to his left hand and swiped at the sweat beading on his forehead. The memory of those final hours in Lewistown was enough to make him feel queasy again. "It was terrible, Leah. And I was no use to you at all. I passed out on the floor. Two orderlies had to use the smelling salts on me while the doctors and nurses were working on you."

"Were you hurt?"

"*Nein.* But what kind of husband am I?" The doubts circling in his mind for four days rushed out. He'd promised himself he wouldn't bother her with them, but this was his old Leah—the one he shared everything with. This was his friend. "I should have been on my feet helping."

"I remember there was a lot of blood, Adam." He heard a rustling sound as she adjusted the phone and said something to his sister. "*Ya*, and Annie just reminded me again, I needed a blood transfusion. Many people would have passed out seeing such a thing."

"Maybe. I wish I could have been stronger."

"He is our strength. Remember? You're the one who found that verse for me, when I was first so miserable with the morning sickness."

Some of the tightness in Adam's chest eased. He had spent hours studying his Bible, searching the Word to ease Leah's suffering. And she had remembered. Perhaps he wasn't such a terrible husband after all. "The Lord God is my strength."

"He will set my feet like the deer," she whispered.

"He will let me walk upon the heights." They finished the passage together.

There was a silence on the line, and this time it was as if they were in the same room. He could picture her there in the odd hospital gown, with her *kapp* fixed on her head. Annie would have seen to that. He could see her holding the phone, eyes closed, whispering the words with him.

"Now tell me about the engines. Did you finish the big one? The one that gave you so much trouble?"

So he did tell her. He talked about the ones he'd finished and the new ones that had come in. He didn't worry at all about how many minutes they used. Samuel had assured him that it was all the same, the bill didn't change according to time spent on the phone. His heart told him he and Leah needed these moments together. It reminded him of the times they used to spend the evening hours together sitting on the porch. When it was colder, they'd sit by the fire after the meal. He would read *The Budget* and she'd work on some piece of sewing.

Why had they ever stopped?

He couldn't remember, but he vowed to himself when she returned home, he'd do better. When she returned with their *bopplin,* he would not allow the distance to creep into their marriage again.

"You're quiet suddenly. What are you thinking about?" Leah asked.

"About how much I miss you. How glad I'll be when you're home and we're together again, the way we were—the way we should be." His voice had grown stronger. Somehow he had grown stronger during their talk. Leah did that for him. She made him the man he could be—the man he should be.

"I know. This hospital—it is *gut*, and I like my doctors very much. I'll be glad to be home though. I miss the farm, and I miss you. Adam, I understand it's a sin to worry, and I'm trying not to. I want to ask though—"

"Ask anything."

"How will we pay for all of this?"

Adam stood and began pacing. He was grateful the phone was wireless so he wasn't confined. "The auction is already scheduled. It's to be next Saturday."

"So soon?"

"It's perfect, Leah. The area is always busy on Thanksgiving weekend, busy with tourists. I wish you could see . . ." he stopped and his throat tightened as he scanned the items in the barn. It was quite full already. "I wish you could see all that folks have brought. Samuel's barn, there's barely room for the horses, and there's more items to come. The bishop says not to worry. The auction will raise plenty, and our medical fund already had a good balance."

"I wish we didn't have to—"

Adam stopped her. "It is difficult to accept help from others. I know, but this is our way. Samuel, your father, and Bishop Levi have met with me twice. To pray and to answer any questions about how this works. At first, I was hesitant as well. But think of all the times we have helped others. Also, it is biblical for all of the community to minister to our children—and to us—in our time of need."

There was a long silence. He wondered if she was crying. He wished he could be there, to hold her in his arms. Phones were useful to a point, good for an emergency, but they would never replace being physically present for the one you love.

"You are right. I wish I could be there, and please . . . please thank them for me."

"You can thank them yourself, when you come home with the *bopplin*."

"The doctors say two more weeks and our children will be born."

"And I will be there. Focus on being stronger, tell the babies I love them, and I will see all of you very soon."

He was about to disconnect the small phone when Leah stopped him, and told him that the doctor knew the sexes of the babies. Did he want to know?

Did he?

"Do you, Leah?"

"It's as if I know them already, carrying them inside me all this time. And it seems unnatural to find out beforehand from some fancy medical test. It doesn't seem our way. Do I sound silly?"

"Not at all. Tell the doctor we will wait. Besides, Belinda has already told us what they are—I'll take her word."

His wife's laughter followed him out of the barn and into the cold. He climbed the steps to Samuel's house and updated him on Leah's condition. Where previously he would have hurried home, he accepted the cup of *kaffi*. They discussed the plans for the following week, and they prayed together over his family. He'd always liked Samuel, but he'd never felt as close to the older man as he did in the last week. Not only did Samuel understand what he was going through, but he'd shown no resentment about Annie staying at Mercy Hospital with Leah. Adam understood what a sacrifice Samuel was making—how much he must miss her and even what extra work it was for him around their home. But Samuel never mentioned it. When Adam brought it up, he'd slapped him on the back and made a joke about how they both would lose weight if it weren't for their sisters' cooking they brought by regularly.

It was dark by the time Adam turned his buggy toward home, but he barely noticed it or the cold. Instead, he remembered the laughter in Leah's voice. He was surrounded by it and the warmth of his family—all of his family.

As he turned down his lane, his thoughts returned to Leah's question, about whether he wanted to know if the babies were girls or boys. Belinda had told them the last time she'd examined Leah, before that terrible night on the bathroom floor, that both were boys. At the time, he'd practically rolled his eyes. Since, he'd grown closer to their midwife—not just from travelling with her to Lewiston and then on the long drive to and from Philadelphia. He'd grown closer because they'd passed through the shadow of fear, if not death, together.

Somehow, if Belinda said the children were boys, then he believed her. She'd also winked and said she was right 75 percent of the time. Pretty good odds.

She would drive him to the hospital again, when the babies were scheduled to be born, or sooner if God willed it. He no longer dreaded the long ride. Belinda wouldn't be able to assist in this birth, and it was not what he would have chosen, but he was slowly accepting that God had reasons for every turn their life took.

He prayed each night the doctors who were involved would treat his wife and children like the precious gifts they were. As for Belinda, he hoped they would need her help again, a few years down the road.

It was a marvel he could now think of the future. Just a few weeks ago the present had seemed so dark. But trouble had done that for him. It had given him a perspective on time. This would pass, and their life would resume its normal rhythm. Until it did, they would depend on their friends, family, and faith to see them through.

15

Annie shouldn't have been surprised, but she was. As she walked to Mercy Hospital on Sunday morning, it seemed to her as if God had prepared the way for what was happening. It seemed to her as if God had cleared a path.

Vickie, her landlady, had insisted on sending a paper sack of home-baked goodies for Leah. "It's good to have you back, Annie. Take these to your sister. Tell her I made them from scratch. I know how you miss your family's cooking." Vickie had pulled her into a hug before sending her out into the cold November sunshine.

The city was exactly as she remembered—crowded, even on a Sunday, somewhat dirty, and already Christmas decorations shone brightly from the display windows. Instead of bothering her as they had before, these things affirmed she was here as a visitor. Soon they would be home.

She received the occasional stare because of her plain dress, but nothing rude. When she smiled back, a young child waved at her, and when one couple started to take a picture, a man stepped in front of them. Whether he did it intentionally to explain they preferred not to be photographed or whether it was an accident, Annie didn't know or care. She stepped through the doors of Mercy and breathed out a sigh of relief.

Perhaps God had used her time of *rumspringa* as a preparation for this day. Perhaps He had known, even then, Leah would need this haven.

"Annie. Is it you?" The nurse who stopped in the middle of the lobby and stared at her had once been Annie's best friend. She still sported short hair, though it had been colored a lovely brown in spots, and remained the blonde Annie was used to in others. She was still as slim as ever.

Annie walked straight into Jenny's outstretched arms.

"What are you doing here? Apparently you're not back to work." Jenny's eyes danced with mischief. Nothing had changed but her hair color.

"I'm here with my *schweschder*, actually my *bruder's* wife. She's having twins and had a partial placental abruption—"

"Is she okay?"

"Yes. Fine. She has Dr. Reese."

"One of our best." Jenny pulled her over to an alcove with chairs. "Who is her neonatal doc?"

"Dr. Kamal."

Jenny's smile grew even wider. "We had to fight to get him. A big hospital out West wanted him, but we won. He's been here a year and everyone thinks he walks on water, which I'm beginning to think could be possible. The man has a heart bigger than those gigantic hands."

"We like both doctors very much."

Jenny sat back and studied her. "You're practically glowing, Annie. Let's see. Your last letter told me about your pregnancy, but I didn't realize you were already showing."

Annie placed her hands across the front of her dress. "Barely."

"I can tell."

"Nurses always can."

"So you're staying here in Philly?"

"Yes. Until Leah's babies are born. We're aiming for two more weeks."

"Give me her room number." After she'd written it down, Jenny added, "And where are you rooming?"

"Same place. Vickie had an opening. *Gotte's wille, ya?*"

Jenny cocked her head. "It would seem so. Same as us running into each other, though you would have found me. Right?"

"I would have."

"*Gut*," Jenny pronounced it with Annie's accent. "Now I don't want to be late for my shift. You know how Shelly is. She would love to see you, by the way. Can you stop by later?"

"I'll try."

"Excellent! I'm off on Tuesday. Would you like to have dinner together then?"

"Yes."

Jenny pulled her into one more hug, and Annie was again wrapped in the feeling that God was going before her, preparing the way.

When she reached Leah's room, the bed was empty. Though she knew she was in the right place, she backtracked into the hall and checked the number on the door.

"She's three doors down," Penny said as she passed her in the hall. "Mrs. Grant's room."

She nodded toward the end of the hall.

Annie gave her a questioning look, but Penny shrugged and offered no explanation. When she reached the room, she tapped lightly on the door. The scene before her shouldn't have surprised her. It wasn't as if Leah had ever been one to sit still. When Annie had first come home, when she'd returned from Mercy to care for her dad, she'd found Leah helping at her home. It was in her nature to care for others.

She was sitting beside an older black woman. Annie would put the woman's age close to forty. She was also near her due date from the size of her abdomen. Leah had her Bible open on her lap and was reading from Galatians, chapter five.

"*Gudemariye*, Annie."

"And to you, Leah." Annie shifted her package from Vickie, which thankfully had enough for three, and her coat and scarf to her left arm. "Having church without me?"

"Actually we are. Mrs. Grant—"

"Alice."

"Alice was saying how she wished she could attend the service downstairs."

"They won't let us. Say it's not safe for our babies. Back home I'd be scrubbing floors and cooking, though not today, of course. Today I'd be singing and praising." The woman's arms came up as she spoke, and she shook one hand as if she were holding a tambourine.

"I thought we might share some Scripture together, the three of us."

"*Gut* idea, and then I have some treats from Vickie." Annie rattled the bag. "Now, what have I missed from Paul's letter?"

So they read through the fifth chapter and into the sixth. They also prayed together. Between them, six children would be ushered into the world in the next few months. Alice was pregnant with triplets and had three to four more weeks of bed rest. Their faith was different in some ways. Alice was a Baptist, and she had spoken several times about missing the praise music in her church with its tambourine, drums, and piano. During Amish services, the only music was their voices. Regardless, the cornerstone of their beliefs was the same—the birth, death and resurrection of Christ.

By the time they walked down the corridor back to Leah's room, it was plain she was tired, but the visit had obviously been good for her.

"It helps to hear someone else's problems," she admitted.

"And to have another person to pray for."

"*Ya.* Imagine three small babies to take home and care for. Plus she has no community to hold an auction, to pay for her bills."

"She has health insurance," Annie pointed out.

"We spoke of that a little. She had heard that Amish don't believe in purchasing insurance, and I explained to her how we depend on each other rather than on a corporation to provide our needs. Her insurance will pay for the bulk of her bill, but she will still have to pay a huge out-of-pocket amount. That's an appropriate term, Annie, because the sum will empty their pockets."

"Yet, we can believe and are assured that *Gotte*, possibly through their church, will provide for them."

Leah stared out the window. "Our lives are so different, but in many ways, what we deal with is the same."

"It's true. I often thought the same thing while I worked here."

Leah rested for the next hour, even dozed a little.

Penny came in and checked on her IV, which would probably be removed the next day, but didn't wake her.

Soon it was time for lunch. After she had eaten and circled the hall again, Annie could see that Leah was growing restless. They read more Scripture, visited with some other mothers, and talked of what their families were doing. But it was the Sabbath, so they didn't work on the quilt.

They waited until the next day, until Monday.

As soon as Annie arrived, Leah was ready for her.

"I'll work on the small squares, the nine patches, while you appliqué."

"Are you sure?"

"Annie . . ." She made the word long, said it in a singsong way like Reba would. "I'm sure. I need something to keep me occupied in this bed. If it's a work of love as you've said, then you should love me enough to let me help."

"*Ya*, all right. You've convinced me."

Annie handed her nine small squares, which she had cut out on Saturday evening—teal, rose, yellow, ivory, pink, lavender, purple, blue, and green. The colors they had chosen together. Leah accepted the needle and thread eagerly.

"You're working on a boy square today?"

"Yes. This pattern always reminds me of Adam." Annie stared down at the pieces in her lap, shaking her head at the memory of Adam in the Lewistown hospital. He'd been so lost. He had reminded her so much of Overall Sam—both with his clothes and with his innocence.

"Annie, I was thinking last night, after you left, about the verses we read from Galatians."

"The same ones you were sharing with Alice."

"*Ya*. I had an idea."

"*Ya?*"

"Remember when Paul talks about how we should be guided by *Gotte's* spirit?" Leah placed the blocks of fabric on the side of her bed. She arranged them in a different order than Annie would have, but they made a nice pattern. She had a good eye for such things.

"Sure, Galatians five, verses twenty-two—"

"And twenty-three. I looked them up again after you left." Leah glanced up, her face all seriousness now. "Paul says if we belong to *Gotte*, and if we are guided by His spirit, then we will produce fruit of the Spirit."

"Love, joy, peace . . ." Annie spread her fingers out on the fabric and ticked off the nine fruits. "Patience, kindness, and goodness."

"*Ya*. Along with faithfulness, gentleness, and self-control. I was thinking that those things, those fruits were missing from my heart the last few months." When Annie tried to interrupt, Leah held up her hand to stop her. "They're back. I feel full and overflowing with them now, but maybe part of the reason I'm here is to focus on the fruit Christ wants me to bear, along with these children."

A slow shiver started up Annie's spine. All things worked to the glory of God. She knew and believed this, but what Leah was saying suddenly felt so right, so obvious, she was certain her revelation was from the Lord.

"Okay, Leah. We'll both focus on it then. What did you have in mind?" She was thinking additional Bible study and more praying. There would be plenty of time to do much of that over the next few weeks, few months actually. But Leah's next words caused them both to grin like schoolgirls.

"The fruits, there are nine, yes?"

"You learned your numbers well," Annie teased.

"And traditionally there are twelve Dutch children on this quilt, but we've changed it to nine—nine children in this nine-patch crib quilt."

The tingling continued as Annie caught on to Leah's idea.

"The story you told Saturday, it was about the first gift, Annie. It was about a child who was saved by love."

Annie didn't speak now. She didn't dare.

"Today perhaps you could tell me a story about joy, as you sew the boy, the boy that reminds you of Adam."

Their eyes met, and Annie knew she couldn't refuse Leah, shouldn't refuse her. She didn't fully understand how a story could implant God's word on their hearts, but she was suddenly sùre that their hours of waiting would be more than sitting and filling time. And the quilt? The quilt would hold a far greater significance than she had ever imagined.

She was halfway done with the Overall Sam—blue pants, green shirt, black hat, and black shoes, before she knew the story Leah needed to hear. It was, to be sure, a story centered around joy.

16

Leah didn't rush Annie to tell her story. She'd thought long and hard all evening the night before. The words in Galatians, the words of Paul, had convicted her heart.

Adam hadn't called on Sunday evening. They'd agreed on Sundays they wouldn't use the telephone, unless it was an emergency. How she'd missed hearing his voice! Almost as much as she missed his hand in hers, his smile in the morning, his body next to hers when she lay down in the evening.

All of which reminded her of how unnatural the last few months had been. She'd allowed herself to become withdrawn. There was no excuse for it. The children in her womb were a cause for the fruits Paul spoke of—for love and joy and peace. She had wasted precious weeks, whole months actually, dwelling in insecurity. It was easy enough to mark her sins in the verses preceding those fruits. Fighting, obsession, losing her temper, conflict, selfishness . . . Paul might as well have written her name on the page.

So she'd prayed, asked forgiveness and focused on the next verses, on the type of wife, and yes, mother, she should be. God had calmed her heart, assured her she was not that old person. She was a new person and had been since the day she'd stood before the church, confessed her faith in Christ, and felt the baptismal waters flow over her head.

She would speak to Adam about it all tonight. She could hardly wait for the phone beside her bed to ring. She had so much to tell him, but mostly . . . mostly she wanted to ask and receive his forgiveness.

As she sewed the small squares together and waited for Annie's story, she marveled that she could feel so renewed in only a matter of a few hours. But then their God was a God of miracles, was He not? And the fact her babies hadn't yet been born was proof.

Annie paused in the middle of sewing Overall Sam's suspenders atop his shirt. She glanced up at Leah and smiled, then stood and refilled Leah's glass of water.

"*Danki*," Leah said. She was drinking more now that the IV was out, but it was good to have free movement of both arms.

"*Gem gschehne.*" Annie crossed over to the window and stared down below at the busy street. The skies had turned cloudy. Perhaps it would snow.

Leah wondered what a snowy Philadelphia would look like. Would it be any prettier? Certainly, it still would not be close to the beauty of their fields and barns and trees when covered with snow.

"Quite the task you've given us, Leah." Annie smiled. "But perhaps if we take it one story at a time . . ."

"*Gotte* will provide," Leah finished.

"Indeed." Annie moved back to her chair and picked up the square she'd been working on. Overall Sam was half-sewn.

Leah thought she'd continue working on the appliqué, but instead she sat, held it in her lap, and began to tell her story, a story of joy, though Leah soon found even those stories have corners that are bittersweet.

—∞∞∞—

I had been helping Belinda with her midwifery duties for almost six months. This was after I'd become engaged to Samuel and a few weeks before we were married. Belinda was called over to help with a birthing in the next district and she asked me to go along. I'm sure she had some idea of the troubles we would face, but they didn't come from the mother or the newborn.

When the father contacted Belinda, he said the mother's pains were strong and close together. Belinda had seen the mother regularly and she'd taken the woman to the doctor twice. Everything was cleared for a home birth. We arrived in plenty of time, but the moment the father stepped from the house—it was in the fall and leaves were blowing every direction—the moment I saw him, I knew something was terribly wrong.

His right arm was the one he'd lost in a farming accident. It had been amputated above the elbow. His wife sewed his shirts so the sleeves made a pocket of sorts for his stump to fit into. I asked Samuel about that later. He said some amputees prefer to keep what's left of their limb covered.

The stump wasn't the problem though. He was long healed of that. The accident had been two years before. However, this man's face, the emotions playing there, they were stormier than the winds tossing the leaves back and forth. He directed Belinda where to park her little car, then trudged straight into the barn.

I had assisted Belinda in nineteen births by then. Josiah was to be our twentieth. I'd never seen a father walk away, without asking a single question. I'd seen frightened, fainting, happy, tired, all sorts of emotions. But I'd never seen a father like Josiah's.

We went inside and the birth was straightforward. Everything was as it should have been, though the mother was alone, and I thought that was odd. Someone had laid out all we needed, and the husband had been with her when we arrived. Our method was for me to stay near the top of the bed and coach the mom and Belinda would catch the boppli. Once the baby arrived, I'd clean up the infant and perform the APGAR test. You and I have talked about that—an APGAR score determines Appearance, Pulse, Grimace, Activity, and Respiration. It's one of my favorite parts of delivery, assessing these new ones. In the meantime, Belinda took care of delivering the placenta and sewing up mom if need be.

That day everything went normally. The birth was easy, though it was the mom's first, and Josiah's score was a nice 8-9. I had bundled him in his blanket and placed him next to his mother's breast when Belinda whispered she needed to leave for a moment. Through the bedroom window, I saw her bowing into the wind, covering the distance between the house and the barn. She was gone for maybe ten minutes. When she came back, the husband was with her, though I couldn't see that there had been any change in his temperament.

She asked me to step out of the room, which was a first. I always stay with the mom the hours immediately following a birth. I went into the kitchen, made tea for everyone, and as time dragged on, also put in a batch of biscuits.

One time, just once, I thought I heard the father shout, but it could have been a tree branch against the top of the roof. I don't mind saying, my heart nearly jumped out of my chest.

When Belinda came out of the room, she told me I could go in and finish showing mom how to breastfeed. I don't know what I expected when I walked back in that room, but I did not expect to see dad, sitting beside his wife, holding his newborn son in the crook of his one gut arm. Belinda didn't speak of it on the way home, and I didn't think it was my place to ask.

Two years later though, last month, actually, I was in town with Samuel and I saw the whole family—all three of them. I wouldn't have recognized them, except dad had on the same kind of shirt, right sleeve sewn above the elbow.

The boy, Josiah, must have recently turned two, and he looked like Overall Sam. He wore these very same clothes if I remember right, and he was walking between his mom and dad—holding on to each with one hand. Mom was pregnant again, if my eye saw correctly.

We all said hello, then Josiah pulled the mother over to a window display a few doors down. Samuel excused himself to pick up something in the post office, which left me standing with the dat.

"I want to apologize," he said. "I was consumed by many things the day you came to my home, the day Josiah was born. I didn't treat you with kindness, and I've regretted that."

It was as if I was speaking to a different man. I remarked on what a beautiful boy Josiah was.

"Ya." I thought he would stop with that, but he scrubbed his hand over his face and pushed on. "I don't know why Gotte allowed the accident that took my arm. Belinda was right though, I can still be a gut dat."

His laugh was full and I can still remember the way he ran his fingers through his beard, the fingers of his left hand. "There hasn't been a single thing I haven't been able to do for my son, and what a blessing he is, Annie. He's the joy of my life—my son is. Gotte is gut, yes?"

Then he turned and strolled away, scooping up his son and dropping him on his shoulder.

<hr />

Leah sat with the squares spread out across her lap, six sewn together and three still waiting. She was back in their small town, walking down the sidewalk with Annie, seeing Josiah riding high on his father's shoulder.

"I don't know what Belinda said to him in the barn, but somehow she took away his fear and reminded him of the joy *Gotte* had in store for him." Annie had resumed her sewing halfway through her story. Now she pulled the last stitch through and tied it off. "It's amazing what joy a child can bring to a life, what places a child can heal—if we let them."

"What do you think they were doing in the bedroom? When you were making tea?"

"Knowing Belinda? I suspect she was showing him how to change a diaper with one arm. Belinda's big on fathers helping with such things." Annie stood as the nurse's aide walked in to check on Leah.

The rest of the afternoon was busy.

She was surprised when one of the volunteers delivered two stuffed bears—both a soft light brown, but one wore a pale yellow ribbon and the other a pastel green.

"The card says they're *from Shelly and the gang.* Who is that, Annie?"

"My former boss when I worked here at Mercy. I forgot to tell you that I ran into my old roommate yesterday."

"The one you were close friends with?"

"*Ya*, Jenny. She wanted me to go to dinner with her tomorrow evening, but I'll only go if you're feeling well."

"I'm fine. You've been with me every waking moment since I arrived. Take some time and visit with your *freind.* I'll crochet a little, and maybe after Adam calls I'll go down and visit with Mrs. Grant."

"Are you sure?"

"More than sure."

Jenny actually stopped by before Leah had her evening meal. It was fun to hear some of the stories about Annie being a young nurse, the tasks she didn't like to do, and how some of the men would flirt with her.

"Do you remember Jeffrey?" Jenny asked.

"I do."

Leah was surprised to see Annie blush as she stuffed her quilting into her bag and prepared to go.

"He teased me every day. I was so young then, or I would have told him to stop. Instead I avoided him, which made it worse."

"He had a crush on you, Annie. You had no idea how charming you were." Jenny and Leah both laughed as Annie rolled her eyes. "Anyway, Jeffrey is married now with four children of his own."

"Four? How did that happen? I haven't been away that long!"

"He moved up to this floor actually. There was a young woman, a widow, who was having triplets, and well—the rest is as the movies . . . oops, guess you don't watch those. It's as the stories go! They fell in love, he asked, she said yes, and two years later they had another child of their own. They moved to San Francisco to be closer to his parents. Needed some help with the crew of girls."

"All girls?" Leah asked.

"All girls. Jeffrey is going to have his hands full." Jenny reached her arms around Leah and gave her a nice, lingering hug. "Do what the nurses say, love. Promise?"

"Of course."

"She's sweeter than you are, Annie."

"I told you so."

Annie hugged her too. "The number for my boarding house is right next to the phone."

"*Ya.* You told me last night."

"I suppose I did."

Leah watched them go, and she was surprised she didn't feel alone. Annie was leaving early so she could walk with Jenny, and Adam would be calling in a few minutes. She was ready to have a long chat with him, the talk where she would clear her heart, apologize for the terrible wife she'd been, and ask his forgiveness.

Love and joy.

Those were two fruits she understood very well, and she'd focus on them whenever she felt sad or lonely. Annie had taken the quilting but left the crochet work she'd begun at Lewistown.

Leah ran her hands over her stomach, said a prayer for the children, a prayer that they would remain in her womb, growing and thriving for another twelve days. Glancing at the clock, she figured it would be another half hour before Adam called. So she picked up Annie's yarn, and she set to work.

17

Adam gazed at the bounty of food cooked and placed around his mother's kitchen. The sight was nearly as beautiful as the snow-covered fields beyond the window. He should feel thankful. It was Thanksgiving, after all. He was appreciative of all his sisters and mother had done to make the day special.

But he didn't feel hungry.

Hanging toward the back of the line, he was surprised when his mother tapped him on the shoulder. "Something wrong, dear?"

"*Nein*. I just, you know, thought I'd let everyone else go first."

Rebekah gave him her look, the I-know-you-better look, and he shrugged.

"Guess I don't have much appetite to tell you the truth. I know you worked hard, and I am grateful for all you've done—"

"Stop right there. Are you worried about the auction Saturday?"

"*Nein*. Everything is ready."

Rebekah squeezed his arm. "Ready and overflowing. We've had to start putting things in our barn as well as Samuel's."

"I know, and I am grateful. It's not that at all. It's—"

"You're missing Leah, plain as the chocolate on my cake. Who can blame you?"

Adam stepped out of the way as Reba dodged past him, trying to grab something out of Trevor's hand. Though Trevor Gray was an *Englischer*, the family was growing accustomed to having him around. He was certainly the best vet in town, in Adam's opinion, and it was obvious they were sweet on one another. The fact that Trevor wasn't Amish, well, Adam had a feeling his father would say that was in God's hands.

"Thanks, *mamm*. I'm glad you understand. I will try to eat something though. Maybe later."

"Have you talked to her today?"

Adam shook his head, his heart tightening as he remembered their conversations the last few nights. "I'll call her this evening."

Rebekah waited, but when he didn't add anything else, she pressed on. "I know you've spoken with her every evening. Samuel told Charity, who told me. I also know Leah's feeling well and the *bopplin* are doing fine. So why the look?"

"Does nothing get past you?"

"Not if I can help it. Not concerning my children. You'll understand that soon."

Adam glanced around. The room was full, and the folks somewhat loud, thanks to all the conversations that began as soon as their time of silent prayer had passed. No one but his mother was paying attention to him. Even Samuel's sister, Rachel, and his *Onkel* Eli were deep in conversation—which seemed to be a civil discussion for once. What was that about? Regardless, it was doubtful anyone would hear what Adam said to his mom. He didn't mind sharing his private life with his entire family, but this still felt personal and . . . well, raw.

"When I called Leah on Monday night . . ." He shook his head, still unable to believe all his wife had said. "*She* apologized to *me* for not being the kind of *fraa* she should be. There she is, in the hospital, far from home, and she's asking my forgiveness."

Rebekah smiled. "She's a *gut* girl, Leah is. I always said so."

"That's it?"

"Son, when a woman apologizes, accept it, say *danki*, and move on."

"But I'm the one who should be asking her forgiveness."

"Did you?"

"*Ya*, I did—"

"*Gut!* Sounds like you two have made up proper."

"*Mamm*, it's not that simple."

"What's not that simple?" Samuel sat down at the table, holding a plate heaped with food that smelled as if it came from heaven's kitchen.

"Leah apologized to Adam, and he's feeling guilty about it."

Samuel's eyebrows raised a fraction of an inch, but he didn't comment. Instead, he spread his napkin across his lap and dug into his baked chicken. Adam had wanted to broach the topic with Samuel. His brother-in-law was married to Annie, so no doubt he knew something about women and apologies, but Adam hadn't found the right time to bring up the subject.

Adam pulled out the chair next to him.

"*Mamm* says I should accept the apology and move on, but I don't know." Adam ran his hand through his hair, causing Charity to smile at him from the other end of the table. She pantomimed holding her hair above her head and cutting it with a pair of scissors. He nodded his understanding. He'd been meaning to let her cut his hair before he headed back to Philadelphia. It was sticking in his collar again.

"And?" Samuel asked.

"And it feels inadequate, just moving on. I was in the wrong as much, actually more, than she was. We both had been acting immature and somewhat selfish." The last word came out mumbled as he stared down at the wooden table. It still hurt to admit, to remember, what a fool he'd been when Leah was here. Now she was gone and he'd do anything to have her back by his side.

"Let me see if I have this right." Samuel raised his fork, using it to accentuate his points. "You both apologized, both agree you were fools, but now you feel as if you should do something more—"

"*Ya. Ya*, that's it."

Samuel dug back into the celery casserole as Rebekah beamed at the two men. "This is nice. I like Thanksgiving when families are together."

"*Mamm*, we're together every week."

"I know. Isn't it nice?"

She patted him on the back and moved over to where Charity and David were sitting together.

"Maybe *Gotte's* spirit is urging you to do something special, Adam. You have a little time on your hands, I'm guessing."

"A little. I'm busy in the shop, but the evenings, well, the nights are lonely as I'm sure you know."

"I do." Samuel wiggled his eyebrows and forked a piece of ham. The man's appetite was causing Adam's stomach to growl. "It's why I'm working on a special project for Annie. I finished her Christmas gift a month ago, but I miss her, and I might as well channel those feelings into a special gift for her."

"Okay. So it's not exactly a repentance gift."

"*Nein*. It's a gift of love, something to express your affection."

"Why didn't I think of that?"

"You're young." Samuel broke a roll in half, releasing steam into the air between them, and added a pat of butter to it. "Can't be expected to think of everything."

"I'm not that young."

"You're not that old."

"Who's old?" Jacob asked, sitting down with a plate heaped with food.

"Did you all leave anything to eat in the kitchen?" Adam asked.

"Perhaps a little, but he who waits last—"

"Is in danger of starving," Samuel finished with a wink.

Adam groaned. The women in his family sometimes quoted proverbs. The men in his family usually quoted nonsense, though in this case they could be right.

He stood and made his way to the kitchen, happy to see there was plenty of food left. As he filled his plate, it occurred to him there was something he could make for Leah. Something she had once asked him for, but he'd told her he was too busy. The question was, could he complete it in the next week?

Certainly he could try. He'd begin this evening, after he used Samuel's phone to speak with Leah—something he found he was looking forward to even more than his *mamm's* pumpkin pie.

<hr>

Annie was surprised when Dr. Kamal walked into Leah's room after they'd finished their Thanksgiving meal. Most doctors did not do rounds on holidays, and Leah had been doing well for several days. The heart rate for both babies was good, and the contractions had not resumed.

She and Leah had taken out the quilting, something they hadn't done since Monday—the week had sped away from them. Annie was learning, surrounded by so many women carrying precious children who were under critical care, that what day the quilt was finished wasn't the important thing. Leah's vision of the quilt had helped calm Annie's nerves over the exact finish date and whether they'd be done by the end of the next week, when the babies would probably deliver.

Annie wanted to begin another Sunbonnet Sue, her apron a light teal on top of a darker green dress. Leah worked on another nine-patch square. They'd divided up the material and pulled out their needle and thread when Dr. Kamal walked into the room.

"I'm in time for the quilting bee." His voice was a combination of bass baritone and sweet molasses.

But why had he stopped by, on a holiday?

"You're probably wondering why I'm here on this lovely, festive afternoon. In my country, Africa,"—as he said the word he rolled the syllables as if he were playing an instrument, like the musicians who came to the town festival—"We do celebrate to the Lord with Thanksgiving, but on a different day. It's difficult for an old man like me to adjust to new ways when it comes to family celebrations."

He smiled broadly and walked forward. "May I touch the babies today, Miss Leah?"

She nodded, and he put his hands on her stomach, moving them around, as if he could tell more by that than he could by studying her chart—which he had done standing outside the door. "Yes, we celebrate to God . . . some to the gods of old, to the god of the harvest, but more and more Christianity is coming to Africa. It is good. The celebrations of old continue, the harvest celebrations, but now the people, they call out Yahweh's name."

He stepped back and Annie pulled up the covers over Leah's stomach. "This quilt you are making, it is for the babies?"

Annie nodded, Leah nodded, and Dr. Kamal smiled. He sank down into the chair beside Leah's bed. "The women in my country still sew. It's rare for me to see it here though."

Leah fingered the small squares of fabric on her bed. "Quilting is a skill we pass down, from mother to daughter. We sew anything we can, and only purchase what we must."

"That is good, too. It brings you peace, I suspect, working with the needle and thread."

Leah turned her gaze to Annie. They'd been talking about peace, the third fruit of the spirit, both trying to think of a story that might match the Sunbonnet Sue Annie was beginning to appliqué.

"Leah's looking at you oddly because we are telling stories as we stitch the quilt."

"One story for each Dutch child," Leah explained.

"And what is today's story about?"

"We were stuck," Annie admitted. "We both were trying to think of a story about a girl."

She positioned the dress and the bonnet—pieces she was about to appliqué—on her square.

"A girl who has something to do with *peace*." Leah emphasized the word as if it were some rare quality. "In truth, both Annie and I were a little unruly as children."

Dr. Kamal's smile widened. "Hard to imagine."

He leaned forward, black forearms braced against his white lab coat. "I might have the right story for you though. When I saw you sewing, I thought of this child. Her name was Nailah. You are my last patient to visit today. If you have the time, I will tell you about her. It isn't a long story, but perhaps it will serve for your purpose and even, I think, be appropriate for this day."

Annie set aside her sewing and reached to put up Leah's, but Dr. Kamal protested. "No, no. You can sew and listen. Continue, please."

So he spoke, with his deep lyrical voice, and they heard the story of Nailah, the African girl.

Nailah's family lived in a modest home in a village in western Africa, in Ghana. There they have the Yam Festival. It's also called Homowo or To Hoot at Hunger. Famine is still a real problem and food considered a blessing, and because of this the people celebrate each September. The rainy season is ending and the crops are ready to harvest. So you see, it is very much like our Thanksgiving here.

Nailah was probably eight years old that year, and I was a young doctor—there was no white in my hair yet! Her mother was near-ing the time to give birth to her second child, and both she and her husband prayed fervently it would be a boy. In Africa, it is still important for families to have a male child, though this family had converted to Christianity and they reminded me each time I visited any healthy child would be a blessing.

In those days births were at home, much as they are in your community, yes? Each time I came to the home, Nailah would be patiently waiting by the front door, in the small amount of shade afforded by a vendor stand her father had made. Though she was young, she could weave baskets with skill, and she would be there waiting and weaving.

I would say hello, and go in to check on her mother. She would nod solemnly but not speak until I was on my way out. Then she would ask me, "Is my mother's time near? Will my brother be born soon?"

Nailah understood we didn't know if her mother was to have a girl or boy, but always her question was the same, and always my answer was the same—that only God knew the time and place of our comings and goings. I expected her to persist, but each time she would say, "Thank you very much, Dr. Kamal," though of course she said it in her native tongue.

As her mother's time drew near, the Festival of the Yams began. The streets were filled with people watching the parade, singing songs, dancing and drumming. The crops had been good that year, and the celebration was . . . how do you say? Over the top! The day Nailah's mother went into labor, I noticed there were no baskets left in the little girl's booth. She had sold every one, for all the women of the village had dug up the yams the day before and had carried them home in baskets on top of their heads. And though Nailah could have joined in the festivities, or even gone into the house to sit in comfort, she remained in her booth as if it were any other workday.

When I asked her about that, she said, "My mother is laboring, so I will labor as well."

"And when the babe is born?" I asked.

"Then we will celebrate together." Her eyes were serious and her tone even. She reminded me she would be outside praying to our God, Yahweh, for as many hours as it took for her brother to enter this world from the heavenly one.

It was one of my more difficult home births. Perhaps that is why I remember, but I like to think God has placed the family in my heart because of Nailah, because of the peace that child embodied and her strong belief.

The morning sun had risen on the next day, the second day of the festival, when I walked back out the front door. The father, he had wept and prayed through the entire night. Perhaps his prayers had saved the mother—who survived, but wouldn't bear more children. He sent me out to fetch Nailah, to bring her in to meet her little brother.

She lay curled in the corner of her booth. Four or five baskets were stacked at her feet, evidence of how she had spent her night. It was plain she was awake though. Her eyes sought mine as soon as I trudged around the corner.

"Does he look like me?" she asked. Those were her first words. She didn't ask if it was a boy or if he was well. Her faith had long covered those questions.

"Perhaps in the eyes. Yes, I think he does."

She jumped to her feet and threw her arms around my neck. Squeezing tightly, she whispered, "May God's angels ever be with you."

And then she was gone, running into the house, her sandals slapping against the hard-packed dirt yard.

———

"Did you ever see her again?" Annie asked.

"I didn't. Soon I was called back to Johannesburg, where I had done my residency. Not long after that, my wife and I made the decision to move to the United States, and I received even more training."

"She's a woman now," Leah whispered.

"Yes, I suppose she is." Dr. Kamal stood. "And one day your children will be grown as well. Perhaps they will ride to Philadelphia on a bus, and see an old black man from Africa, one who was given the privilege of helping them into this world."

He paused, touched Leah's stomach once more and said, "A blessed Thanksgiving to you both."

After he'd left the room, Annie focused on finishing her Sunbonnet Sue. When Leah had clipped the thread to her nine squares, she placed it on the side of the bed and sighed. "He can tell a story."

"That he can," Annie agreed.

"Love, joy, and peace."

"I can hardly wait to hear patience." Annie folded their quilt pieces and placed them in her bag.

Six quilt squares to go, and eight days until Leah's babies would be born.

18

Adam stood beside Charity looking at the rows and rows of quilts hung on the clotheslines behind Annie and Samuel's house. The one thing more surprising than the quantity of quilts was the amount of cars and buggies lining the lane.

"Where did they all come from, Charity?"

"The quilts or the people?" She bumped him with her shoulder, a slow smile spreading across her face.

"The quilts. Surely you women didn't sew them all since Leah was taken to the hospital."

"*Nein*. Women quilt. Amish women quilt constantly. Tell me you haven't noticed this."

Adam scuffed his work boot against the ground, grateful that the day had dawned sunny and not too cold. The little snow they'd had on Thanksgiving eve had melted. "So you're saying—"

"Every woman I know has three or four quilts put back, for such a time as this."

"And then they—"

"They give them, Adam." Charity pulled the strings of her prayer *kapp* forward, then ran her fingers from the top of the string to the bottom as she studied him. "Think of it as money in the bank—put back for an emergency. This is an emergency, and everyone is happy to help. Oh, look at the woman in red heels fingering *mamm's* double wedding ring. I should go and see if she wants to make an offer."

His sister was off before he could say another word. Nor did he have time to be alone. His *Onkel* Eli replaced her before Adam was able to take a single step.

"Nice to see the community pulling together." Eli slipped his thumbs under his overalls. Though the day was cool, he wore no coat, only a long-sleeved blue shirt and black suspenders with his customary black pants. "And a real blessing this happened at a time that there are so many tourists in the area."

Adam studied him, waiting.

"Think, Son. If the babes had been born sick, and we'd had the auction after Christmas? Not many tourists on a cold, snowy January Saturday. I'm sure *Gotte* would have provided, mind you." Eli nodded toward Rachel. "Could be He's even using this to soften the hearts of others among us."

"You think so?"

"She closed down her shop to help today. Asked me to pick her and the boys up. Said if folks wanted to spend their dollars, they could spend them here. Doesn't sound like the entrepreneur I've come to—" Eli stopped himself, looked left and then right, as if to see who might be listening. "To tell you the truth, Adam, she didn't sound at all like the *business woman* I've come to care for."

"You? And Rachel?"

"Don't have to publish it in the paper." Eli grinned and rocked back on his heels. "I figured being a newly married man yourself, you'd understand."

"But . . . Rachel?"

"Never limit yourself to looking on the outside, Son. Though she's a beautiful woman, I understand she's presented a hard shell to the world. I think it may be because of the difficult past she's had. Rachel has shared a little of her history with me the last few weeks."

As they watched, Rachel knelt beside both of her sons and spoke with them, pointing toward the area where Rebekah was accepting payment for goods. Jacob was directing children to help folks carry their purchases back to their cars and buggies. Matt and Zeke nodded once, and then hurried toward Adam's parents. Rachel stood, then scanned the crowd until her eyes found Eli. Instead of walking toward him, she smiled and turned to help the women preparing lunch.

Adam shook his head. "I suppose I never thought of you, well, of you . . ."

Eli's grin was answer enough. "I had begun to wonder myself, if *Gotte* had such plans for me. It would seem maybe he was allowing me to wait, so I could be a father to those two boys."

"Not that I've asked yet," he added.

"Oh." Adam couldn't think of what else to say. His head was spinning. His *Onkel* Eli? Married? To Rachel?

"I should go and help those young children with my toys. They seem at a loss as to where the *on* button is for a pull horse." His laughter followed him as he walked away.

Wow. Adam had a lot to talk to Leah about when he called her. He was sure there was something serious going on between Charity and David, and possibly Reba and Trent, and now Eli and Rachel. Not to mention describing all the people who had shown up for the auction. How he wished his wife could be here.

He trudged toward the barn where the men had set up the food tables, when his youngest sister joined him.

"Bake sale is going well," Reba said. "And we've nearly sold out of tickets for the luncheon."

"It's . . . a lot to take in." He waved one arm toward the tables holding crafts, including a good deal of *Onkel* Eli's wooden toys. With the other hand, he pointed at the pen of animals. "Are we auctioning those goats and sheep?"

"*Ya.* Folks love to see an animal auction. Adam Weaver, you act as if this was your first benefit auction."

"Honestly, I didn't pay much attention before. The last few years, I was more interested in sneaking off alone . . ." He stopped suddenly, realizing who he was talking to—his little sister!

Reba's laughter pealed across the yard, mingling with the sounds coming from the dozens of children, Amish and *Englisch*. "You think I didn't figure that out? Tell me something new about my *bruder*, something worthy to be published in *The Budget*."

"I wouldn't want to be a bad influence on you, is all. And don't think I haven't seen the way you look at Trent. He's your boss, you know, and an *Englischer* to boot."

Reba stepped closer, looping her arm through his. "What does love feel like, Adam?"

Instead of answering, Adam groaned.

"Does it make your stomach hurt a little? Does it make you want to sing sometimes, and other times long to hold your head in your hands? Is that what love is like?"

"If you want to know about love, read Paul's first letter to the Corinthians."

"*Ya,* I know. It's patient, kind. It doesn't envy or boast."

"Fine. You know the scripture. Then you know you should be thinking of someone from within our own community of faith."

Reba pulled him to a stop, right next to the baked goods table. "He's speaking to the bishop, Adam. About converting."

"Reba, you know how difficult that is. Since I've been a *kind*, only three, no, four people have tried and all have failed."

Smiling so brightly Adam's heart actually hurt for her, Reba continued pulling him down the rows of tables. "All the more reason for us to pray for him, dear *bruder*. Now, I want you to try some of my cookies."

"You baked?"

"Yes. It's the first time in years, and I'm afraid to auction them before they've been sampled by humans."

⸺⸺

Annie had expected Monday to pass slowly. The week seemed to stretch out in front of them like a long road.

"I wish we could have been there," Leah admitted.

"*Ya*, but if we were there, probably there would have been no need for an auction."

"True." Leah sighed and stared at her toes. "One of the good things about the hospital bed is I can raise the foot of the bed and see my toes. The swelling has nearly disappeared from my ankles."

"Because you're in bed more."

"*Ya*. My feet almost look normal."

"Some reason you're giggling over there?" Annie was putting the finishing touches on a return letter to Reba. She folded the paper and slipped it into the envelope.

"I was remembering how Adam had to put my shoes on for me. Those were the days."

"Only two weeks ago."

"And by the end of this week, he'll be here. Holding our babies." Leah placed her hands on her stomach.

A few hours earlier, both of her doctors had stopped by. They agreed that Saturday was the prime date for delivery, if she could make it that long—it would mark the end of her thirty-sixth week. There was a possibility she could go longer, but the odds of that were slim and they cautioned against raising her hopes.

"How many more hours until Adam calls?"

"At least three." Annie stood and moved to the side of her bed. "Do you want to walk some more? Or quilt?"

"Let's quilt. I love what we did on Saturday."

Annie pulled out the long strip of quilting. She and Leah had worked on sewing together more nine-patches, then they had connected the three completed doll squares with sashing.

"I love the dark blue and green strips. They add the right amount of color between the white squares." Leah sighed. "And I can imagine draping this over my *boppli*, Annie. I'll think of Paul's letter to the church in Galatians each time I do, and I'll remember our stories. I'm sure I will."

"*Ya.* I have no doubt my memories will be rich every time I pick up my niece or nephew." Running her hand from left to right, she touched the blue Sunbonnet Sue, the blue and green Overall Sam, and the green and teal Sue. "On other quilts, I waited until all of my squares were done to put together any rows."

"It helps to see what the finished piece is going to look like. It helps me be more patient." Leah squinted one eye as she said the last word. "I keep thinking about the doctor's story and the African girl."

Annie pulled more fabric from her bag. "Time to start the top row, yes?"

"Yes! Which means we need another story." Leah pulled the nine squares toward her.

It did Annie's heart good to see how much healthier her sister-in-law had grown since coming to Mercy. Not only physically, though it was a blessing, to be sure. But Leah's emotional, mental, and spiritual state had moved a far distance from where it had been when they'd knelt beside her on the floor of her bathroom. Certainly, God had used this time for healing. His ways were above their ways. Indeed they were.

Annie pulled the thread through her needle, and the needle through her layers of cloth. She had prayed about many things as she prepared for her hospital visit this day. Her visits the last few nights with Jenny had reminded her how important friendships were, whether they existed within a family or outside of one.

Reba's letter and the revelations of her feelings for Trevor were just one more example of how the cords of friendship could stretch and extend beyond where they normally exist. Didn't she know that? Jenny was a perfect example. It had never mattered Jenny was *Englisch*. She'd been a friend when Annie needed one.

Would those cords of friendship stretch as far as marriage for Reba? Could Trevor withstand the sacrifice of converting to their faith? Reba had confessed she had no desire to leave the Amish way, and Trevor didn't want her to. He was happy living and working among the Amish, and he respected their faith and worship.

Perhaps it would work out this time.

Maybe friendship and love would be enough to help him through the requirements the bishop would put on him.

Other friendships existed inside a family though, even inside a marriage. Watching Leah piece together her nine-patch squares, Annie wondered if this dear girl she'd grown to love realized what a friend she had in Adam.

Clearing her voice, she set down her quilting, poured them both a cup of water, and said, "Perhaps you should tell the story today."

"Me?" Leah's voice squeaked like the gate in their back pasture.

"*Ya.* Tell me a story about Adam."

Leah's brow wrinkled as she focused on the fabric and making her stitches even. She didn't speak for three, four, then five minutes. Annie sat and resumed her own sewing. When Leah started giggling softly, Annie inwardly breathed a sigh of relief.

"Adam is not one who is naturally patient."

"Don't I know it."

"He's more like one of David's donkeys, wanting something the minute he thinks of it. The man is impatient when it's not raining because it should be, and eager for it to stop when the storms come." Leah stopped sewing and looked around the room. "I wonder if maybe it's our age. Sometimes it feels as if we need to hurry things along."

Shaking her head, she resumed sewing. "But there was this time after church service. He didn't know I was watching, and I wasn't spying on him exactly, but I saw him with Rachel's youngest, with Zeke . . ."

19

I had been helping in the serving line, and so I knew Adam hadn't come through. My morning sickness was better that day, for once. Services were at Faith and Aaron Blauch's, and it must have been . . . it must have been in May going on June? Something like that. I remember the days were growing warmer and Noah was running around like a wild pony. That child has grown like a weed, Annie. It's hard to believe he's the first infant you and Samuel brought into the world together.

I'm off my story—you see I don't tell one as well as you do. I'd gone looking for Adam. I was afraid the teenage boys would start through the line a second time and there would be nothing left, so I'd put back a plate for him. My plan was to tell him where it was and let him be.

I came around the corner of the barn and I saw the two of them. Probably you're thinking I should have spoken up or done something to make myself known. Maybe. But at the time, I couldn't. Have you ever stumbled upon a deer and its fawn, Annie? That's what the moment was like. I couldn't move. All I could do was watch, and besides—Zeke had that terrified look on his face, you know the one he gets.

I don't think Rachel beats that child, but perhaps someone has in the past. He freezes and you have to talk him down. We've all seen it, so there's no use looking at me reproachfully. I pray for her and her children same as you do. Pray for their healing and that Gotte will bring a man into her life, though with her sour disposition it doesn't seem likely, does it?

I'm hopping away from my story again.

Zeke was standing there trembling, actually shaking, and it was plain as day why. He was covered in those sticker burrs from head to toe. The child must have rolled in them. I know because I heard Adam say, "How'd you get so many, Zeke?"

Adam, who barely has the patience to groom our own horses properly—he'd rather charm Reba into doing it for him—Adam was squatted down in front of him when I came around the corner. Must have been the way the breeze was stirring, because I could hear every word he said.

"I haven't seen this many sticker burrs since Reba brought home that mongrel dog, named him Patches, and left him in the barn. He got out through a loose board in the sidewall and went out in the pasture. Didn't run away though. Patches knew where the soup bone was coming from. He did manage to roll in the sticker patch and Reba sat out there and combed every single one from the dog's scraggly hair."

Zeke didn't say anything. You know how silent he is. He stood there, in his Sunday clothes, with his hat in his hands and his head bowed as if he were still praying along with Bishop Levi. I could see the back of his neck from where I stood at the corner of the barn, and I started to step out, I did. But then Adam, who had been pulling stickers from the boy's pants, said, "What's wrong, Zeke? Why are you shaking?"

Zeke looked up, and I thought he might speak, but instead he shook his head once and stared back down at the ground.

"Don't worry about it. We won't tell anybody. We'll have these out, in another . . . well, in another hour or so. No harm, no foul as they say in the sports column I sometimes read."

Zeke glanced up again, and Adam laughed then.

"You didn't know I like sports? Sure. I keep up with the baseball games the Englischers play, and even sometimes the football. Can't say as I follow the other sports much."

Eventually Zeke held out his arms, and Adam continued pulling out the sticker burrs. They were even in his hair, somehow. You know how those burrs are . . . you can't brush them out, you have to pull, and you have to pull carefully or it can tear the fabric. I happen to know that Rachel didn't notice because later that day, when I'd already hightailed it back to the table and Adam and Zeke had appeared as if nothing at all was wrong, Rachel called him over.

She asked him what he'd been doing, and Zeke only shrugged. He did glance over at Adam, who said, "We were talking sports. Right, Zeke?"

Zeke nodded, because of course it was the truth.

I ran and fetched Adam's plate for him, along with a big glass of lemonade. I knew he must be awful hungry, but when I put it down in front of him he grabbed my hand and started talking about the babies, asking if I thought they would be boys or girls.

Somehow, I knew that day that Adam would be a gut father— not because he's a patient man—believe me, he's not. The next evening, he was outside hollering at one of those engines of his that wouldn't go back together right. No, I think he'll be a gut father because he can find patience, he can call it up out of his heart for a child, and maybe that accounts for more than if he'd had it there all along.

Annie put down her quilt square.

She knew, firsthand, how impatient her brother could be. And yes, she'd also seen the tender side of him—less so lately as the pressure of having a family had begun to take its toll.

She studied Leah. "A wonderful fourth story, and it matches our fourth Dutch child."

She held up the finished appliqué square. The boy wore a purple shirt, blue pants, black shoes, and black hat. They both laughed. Annie pressed her fingertips against the quilt blocks they were putting together. She would always remember the stories of love, joy, peace, and patience—the stories of the fruit of God's spirit. As her mind brushed over each one, she was reassured everything would turn out fine.

The remainder of the afternoon sped by.

Soon Adam was calling, still talking about what a success the auction had been. They had the totals now, and the sale of goods had raised more money than expected. Combined with what was already available in the medical fund, Leah's expected medical expenses and those of the babies shouldn't be a problem. It was a huge burden lifted from everyone's shoulders.

Adam had been full of details on Saturday, and Sunday he hadn't called. This evening he seemed to be telling Leah small tidbits he'd forgotten to relay. Annie knew the moment he began talking about Reba and Trent because Leah sighed and said, "Ya, we know. Annie received a letter from her and has already written back. We'll all pray, Adam."

Annie was relieved to hear the easy way the two spoke with one another. It seemed the tension from previous weeks had vanished.

"Are you sure?" Leah asked into the phone.

Turning abruptly from the window, Annie found a giant grin on Leah's face. "Eli himself told you this?"

"What—"

Leah held up her hand. "*Ya*, I'll tell her . . . I miss you too, Adam . . . Tomorrow night. I'll be here. Where else would I be? . . . Yes, I'll give your love to the babies."

She hung up the phone, not even attempting to hide the wistful sigh. "I miss him."

"Sure you do, but what did he say about Eli?"

"That he's *in lieb*."

"Eli? My *Onkel* Eli?"

"*Ya*. What other Eli do we know in our district? And you'll never guess with whom."

"I'm not going to have to guess, because you're going to tell me." Annie scooted her chair closer. "Tell!"

Leah tapped her chin as if she was suddenly having trouble remembering, but she couldn't hold out for long. "Rachel!"

Annie searched through her mind. Coming up blank, she finally asked, "Rachel who?"

"Rachel, Samuel's *schweschder*!"

"Oh, Leah. I thought there must be another Rachel I couldn't remember. Are you sure?"

"*Ya*. Adam says . . ." Leah shrugged. "Adam says she's different this last week or so, or at least Eli says she's different. Adam admits he hasn't paid much attention."

Different? How different could she be? Annie had been praying for a change of heart in Rachel, had been praying God would bring someone into her life to care for her and show her love. But Eli? If it were true, God certainly did work in mysterious ways.

Leah had already had her dinner, which always came early, same as at home. Annie stayed long enough to help her walk around the floor one more time. It seemed she moved somewhat slower, but then they were both distracted by all they had learned from the phone call. She wondered if she should stay, but Leah shook her head and said she was tired and would go to sleep early.

Annie was aware that the evening hours in a hospital room could drag on and seem to crawl toward morning. If Leah were sleeping though, and she did look more tired than usual, perhaps it would be best for Annie to return to the boarding house.

She was gathering her things to leave when Leah placed her hands on her forehead and groaned.

"*Was iss letz?* Should I call a nurse?"

"*Nein.* It's only my head." Leah sat forward, now cradling her head. "I suddenly have the worst headache."

Annie dropped her bag and her coat and slipped the automatic blood pressure cup onto Leah's arm. Then she pushed the *Call Nurse* button.

"Leah, I want you to sit back, dear. Sit back and take a few deep breaths. The nurse is coming."

"Everything all right in here?"

"Her BP is—"

"I see it." Foster pushed the call button again, his usually cheerful expression was missing as he bustled around the room. His movements were quick and efficient, and they did much to calm Annie's fears.

When someone from the nurse's desk beeped the room, he advised them, "We need to contact Dr. Reese. Stat."

"It hurts, Annie."

"I know it does, honey. They'll give you something very soon."

"Let's put the fetal monitor back on her. Annie, help me slip it around her waist."

Together they worked it under and around Leah. The two lines immediately appeared on the monitor display, and they confirmed what Leah's blood pressure had shown. Both the babies and Leah were in distress.

The head nurse walked in. Her name was Nancy Baxter, and they'd had very little to do with her because Leah had been on intermittent monitoring since her placenta bleed had stopped. Baxter was older, tall, thin, gray-headed, and Annie could tell by one look she'd seen most everything a maternity ward could offer.

"Leah, your blood pressure is very high. That's the reason your head hurts. I want you to take this medicine, lie back, and try to rest." Baxter handed her a small paper cup, the kind Annie had handed to patients a hundred times.

Annie didn't see what was in it, because Baxter was issuing orders.

"Annie, would you draw those blinds, please? We don't want any sights or sounds outside to agitate your sister."

Leah had taken the medicine, but continued groaning from the bed. "I think I might throw up."

"I'd like you to keep that medicine down, Leah. Also, we'll want you to lie on your left side until we say otherwise." Baxter glanced up. "Annie, could you pour a little ginger ale in a cup for her? Perhaps it will settle her stomach while Foster starts a line."

"An IV?" Leah glanced in confusion from Foster on her left to Nurse Baxter on her right.

"Leah, focus on me. It's going to be fine. Do you believe me?"

Leah nodded, though her chin was trembling.

"Your sister Annie caught this very quickly. Your blood pressure was high, too high, but we're bringing it down. I want you to focus on something that will calm you. Can you do that? Think of something peaceful, and try to relax."

"The quilt," Leah whispered.

Annie snatched the bag off the floor and pulled out the single panel they'd completed. "Remember, Leah? Love, joy—"

"And peace. *Ya*." Leah pulled in a deep breath.

"Good girl. Here, sip this."

Leah took a small drink of the ginger ale, placed her hands on top of the quilt panel, and closed her eyes. Annie couldn't make out her words, but she knew that she was praying.

Moments passed as they waited, all eyes glued on the monitor.

"Fetal heartbeats are stabilizing," Foster said.

Baxter was called into the hall by an orderly. When she returned she announced, "Doctor Reese is on her way. Nurse Foster will stay with you until the doctor walks into this room, and he'll call me if there's any change at all."

Touching Annie's arm, she nodded toward the hall.

Once the door to Leah's room had closed behind them, Baxter began, not pausing to give Annie a chance to offer her version of events.

"Normally I don't abide family members touching my equipment, but in this case you did the right thing. As I'm sure you realize, her BP was dangerously high. Dr. Reese ordered a single dose of Methyldopa orally and Labetalol intravenously. I'm not accustomed to sharing such details with individuals who aren't staff; however . . ." she paused to give Annie a once-over, from the top of her *kapp*-covered head to the toes of her sensible shoes. "I've heard things about you, from your former supervisors—good things. And you've proven yourself to be useful here. Sometimes Amish patients can be a problem—no offense."

"None taken."

"I want you to prepare your sister—and her husband—for the likelihood that these babies may come sooner than anticipated."

Annie waited, sensing Nurse Baxter didn't want idle chit-chat from her. She thought for a moment that the floor supervisor was going to dismiss her when the older woman nodded ever so slightly, then Annie remembered she didn't actually work there.

She turned to push back into Leah's room when Baxter called her back. "Although we don't usually allow family to stay overnight, we'll make an exception in this case. Foster will provide whatever you need."

"*Danki*," Annie said, but she wasn't sure Baxter heard her. The woman was already treading softly down the hall, on her way to care for another mother in need.

20

Adam wanted to leave the minute he pressed the END button on Samuel's cell phone, the very second they finished speaking with Annie.

"If you think it's best, we'll find a driver." Samuel studied him from the front porch steps. He'd driven over as soon as he'd heard from Annie, knowing that Adam would need to talk to the women himself.

By the time he'd reached Adam's house, Leah was asleep. There seemed to be no need to waken her, so Annie had repeated what she'd already told Samuel. It did help to hear his wife's condition firsthand.

"I feel as if I should go—now."

"*Ya.* I understand why."

"You're sure the doctors are waiting though."

"They told Annie they'd reassess her condition in the morning. If her blood pressure is at an unsafe level, they'll give her medication to begin labor or possibly schedule a cesarean."

Adam rested his head in his hands and waited for all of the words to make sense. He waited for the fear to retreat. Finally, he stood and stared toward his fields in the pitch-black night.

A cold winter wind had begun to blow as soon as the sun had set. There'd be snow before the week was out, probably a lot of it.

"It's not what we wanted, Samuel. Not how we envisioned this thing to go. But the children are still safe, and so is Leah. That's the important thing."

"Agreed."

"You think I should wait?"

"I think if she's stable in the morning then it could still be Saturday before the twins are born. You'll have travelled there only to stay a few hours and travel back, and—" he bit off the end of the sentence.

"Say it. We've come through too much in the last few months to hold back now."

"Though I don't doubt at all Leah would like to see you." He stood, walked next to him, and placed his hand on his shoulder. "It could be she'll rest more if we aren't there."

Adam scrubbed his hand across his face. He hadn't thought of that, but there was a ring of truth to what Samuel said. "Annie told me the doctors make their rounds at ten."

"Yes."

"I'll be done with my work by then and be at your house."

"And I'll have called Belinda at first light. We'll be sure to have her or another driver ready to go."

Samuel's work boots crunched against the gravel of his drive as he made his way out to his buggy. Growing up, Adam had often wished for a brother. Reba was close, with her love of animals and willingness to follow him into a creek or thicket or deer stand. Charity had been like a second mother, always seeing there was a warm plate of food on the stove if he worked late. And Annie had been his friend, being the closest in age.

Samuel directed his buggy down the lane, and the two small red brake lights blinked, throwing a small reflection on the larger red triangle. He prayed Samuel would find his way safely home, and then he paused and thanked God for sending him the brother he'd always wanted.

As he walked through the house and cleaned up the few dishes in the sink, he continued to pray—for Leah, the children, and the doctors. For Annie and her baby. He prayed for his parents—this time had been difficult for them as well. Praying came more naturally to him after all they'd been through. Before Leah had become pregnant, honestly before she'd gone to Lewistown, he hadn't thought of himself as much of a praying person.

He prayed at church, of course, and he thanked God for his food each meal. He'd never considered himself a praying man though. When it came time for the drawing of lots, when there was a need to elect more leaders within their church, he always secretly hoped it wasn't his name called. He knew he didn't have the spiritual maturity to lead others.

He was still fumbling around trying to find the way himself! But things had changed since Leah's illness. He'd learned to lean on God, since he certainly couldn't lean on his own understanding—he didn't understand any of this!

Now whenever the world grew quiet around him, he found himself falling into an easy conversation with God—thanking Him for all He'd done, asking Him for direction, remembering His word, even pleading for His help.

Certainly good had come out of these times. Though he'd be glad when his wife was home, with his children, and everything returned to normal. As if he knew what being a father was like, or how having babies would change things in their home.

What was normal for a family of four?

As he pulled off his work clothes and set the battery-operated clock to go off an hour early, to go off long before the morning light would touch the edge of his fields, he prayed he would learn what that kind of normal was.

"Give me the chance, Lord. Give us one more day together, and then one more day after that." And with words of blessing for his family on his lips, he fell into a deep sleep.

Leah felt disoriented when she first woke.

She'd become accustomed to the hospital room, but why was the IV back in her arm? And the fetal monitor around her stomach? And Annie sitting in the chair, quilting by the small lamp?

The memories of the last few hours came back to her in a rush, causing her heart to race and sweat to pop out across her brow.

"You're okay." Annie was at her side in seconds. "You and the *bopplin* are fine. Here, take a sip of the water."

Leah allowed the coolness of the drink to settle her nervousness. She pulled in two, then three deep breaths, and noticed when Annie's gaze moved from the heartbeat monitor back to her, a smile tugging at the corners of her lips.

"Are we good in here?" Foster stuck his head in through the door, light from the hallway spilling across the room.

"*Ya.* I believe she was a little confused when she woke is all."

Foster's eyebrows arched. They looked comical contrasted against his extremely short haircut. Leah knew he wouldn't leave until she'd confirmed she was fine.

"I feel better. *Danki.*"

"All right then. Push your button if you need anything. I'm on for another thirty minutes."

Leah remembered most of what had happened since her head had begun to ache, but she was relieved when Annie pulled her chair closer and recounted the evening's events anyway. Her fear had made some of the events loom larger than others. Hearing Annie describe Nurse Baxter, who was quite somber, and Dr. Reese, who had been concerned but not overly so, helped to settle her mind and heart.

"The babies are fine?"

"*Ya.* You can see their heartbeats yourself. The two lines on the display to the right of yours."

Leah watched them for a while. Turning back to Annie, she was surprised to see her quilting again.

"So late?" she teased.

"It's better than the *Englisch* television." Annie shook her head, *kapp* strings flapping against the chair. "I didn't want to leave, and I wasn't ready to sleep myself. I hope the light isn't what woke you."

"*Nein.* I've slept a lot already. Sew away."

She watched as Annie placed the pastel lavender apron on top of the dark purple dress and began to stitch around it.

"You'll have to tell a story though."

"Leah Weaver. You must be kidding. It's nearly eleven at night."

"Never too late for a story. Now let's see—we've covered *love, joy* . . ."

"*Peace, patience,* and . . ." Annie's needle paused in midair.

"You just thought of one! You thought of a story about a girl that has to do with *kindness.*"

"Perhaps I did." Annie resumed her sewing. "I believe the babies will be fine, Leah."

"And so do I." They stared at one another across the bed, across the quilt, across the space of four or five feet, which was actually no space at all.

"So tell me the story." Leah took another sip from the cup of water, then placed both hands on her stomach. She didn't gaze at the monitor any longer. She didn't need to. God was watching over her children.

⁘

When I first left Mifflin County, when I went to live with my aenti, I stayed in her house to finish my homeschooling. You know Amish children only learn through eighth grade, and Englisch children learn through twelfth. I needed to pass the high school equivalency exam to take classes at the local college. Aenti had me take a practice exam, and I did well in Englisch and math. I even managed to pass history—though not as well as I would have liked. Science, though, gave me a lot of trouble. And science is very important if you're interested in nursing. So I had to go back to the beginning.

I tried teaching myself, but it's difficult to educate yourself in a subject you know little about. Finally Aenti found me a tutor—a science teacher from the local high school. She was a single mom. I never learned what happened to her husband, but she had two children. The older girl's name was Hailey and the younger girl's name was Sofia. My story, my story of kindness, is about Sofia.

But first I need to tell you about Hailey. She was my age at that time—beautiful in the way of the Englisch models you will sometimes see on the front of magazines. She didn't have a car—I don't suppose they could afford one—but her freinden did. They would often drop her off or pick her up, never bothering to come into the home. She was always on one of the cellular phones like Samuel has and didn't speak much to her mamm. Mostly she stayed in her room if she was home. Above all she never spoke to her schweschder. Never looked directly at her. I can't say what Hailey was like, because in my three months of caring for the young girl and being tutored by the mother, I never did get to know the teenage girl in any meaningful way.

The young girl, Sofia, I did get to know. She was three years old, only beginning to learn words, and full of life. Her hair was solid blonde curls, and she smiled at nearly everything. When she did cry, over some small bump when she'd fallen down or once when Hailey came in and slammed a door, it was easy enough to distract her with a story or a game. Soon she would be smiling again.

I walked to Sophia's day care in the neighborhood at three in the afternoon and kept her until six when her mother came home. Usually I took a stroller that belonged to the family, and Sophia would sit in it while I pushed her home. Occasionally she would run or walk beside the stroller. Very early I learned Hailey could have done this—she was often home before me since her school let out at two-thirty. Why she didn't I don't know, but as I said, she would have nothing to do with the child.

A few times, when Hailey would go into the kitchen for water—I never saw her actually eat—Sophia would run to her and try to give her a small drawing or share a cookie with her. These times Hailey would not speak sharply to her, but would rather walk away as if Sophia didn't exist. Once the mother was in the room. She had come home, and we were about to begin our tutoring lesson. When this happened, I saw an expression of such pain, remorse I think, pass over her face, that it felt as if one of Reba's critters had scratched me.

No one spoiled Sophia, but she was very attached to what she called her blankie. It was a small square of a blanket, with a satin trim and a rabbit's head. She carried it with her everywhere, and when I washed it she would sit outside the machine and wait for her blankie to come out. She would take it to day care, eat with it, even sleep with it.

I don't know all the details of what happened the day Hailey walked home from school. I had already picked up Sophia—her day care wasn't far from my aenti's house or their own home. It was actually a nice stroll. We'd arrived home, had our snack, and were sitting on a blanket in the front yard. I don't know that Hailey even saw us. I certainly had never seen her walking before, always her freinden had driven her.

Sophia saw her first. She pointed and said, "Hailey home." She never did call her schweschder. Hailey walked into the house, a look of complete devastation on her face. I hurried inside, carrying Sophia. Hailey had never been rude to me, though she also didn't speak to me more than was necessary. I asked her if she was all right, but she didn't seem to hear me. I expected her to go into her room as she always did.

She didn't though.

Instead, she made it to the kitchen, stopped at the icebox where they kept bottled water, and there she sank to the floor. Before I could reach her, Sophia broke away from me. She climbed in her lap, handed her the blankie, and said, "Here, Hailey. Take it."

Hailey stared at the small square of cloth, as if she were seeing it for the first time, but Sophia was working her sister's fingers around it, showing her how to clutch it. Finally when Sophia was sure the blankie wouldn't drop to the floor, she took her two small, chubby hands and placed them on each side of Hailey's face. "It's gut. Ya?"

She said it the Amish way, plain and simple.

I'm telling you there was so much kindness in that child it practically poured from her.

Hailey stared at her for five, six, maybe seven heartbeats. I thought she'd push her off her lap, run to her room, and slam the door again. But instead, she wrapped her arms around Sophia and began to weep.

That's how her mother found us—all three in the kitchen, sitting on the floor.

The next day, the mother called my aenti and said I was ready to take my equivalency exams. She also said I wouldn't need to pick up Sophia anymore and she'd pay through the end of the week since my job was ending so abruptly.

I saw them once though. A week later, I was walking from the grocery store, and I saw Hailey, walking home with Sophia. They were holding hands and Sophia was still carrying her blankie.

~oxxo~

"What happened?" Leah asked. She could practically see the two girls and the younger Annie. "What caused it? People don't change easily, especially teenagers—whether they're Amish or *Englisch*. It's a stubborn age."

"True. *Aenti* learned through some neighbors that there had been a car wreck at lunch that day. The accident seriously injured three siblings, including a teen and two younger children. I suppose it woke Hailey up, caused her to appreciate the family she had."

"But Sophia didn't need waking up."

"*Nein.*" Annie stored her quilting supplies as the hands on the clock moved toward midnight. "I think Sophia is one of those souls who understands the value of each day. She seemed born awake and born to kindness."

Leah didn't protest when Annie rearranged her pillows and encouraged her to close her eyes. The story had caused her to feel sleepy again. As Annie turned off her lamp, leaving a mere sliver of light from the bathroom, Leah wondered if her mind would dwell on the tragedy in the story—on the three who had been injured. Had they recovered? Or had they died? She had heard her own *mamm* say when a young person died in their own community, "Her life was complete." Her parents and her faith had taught her to view death not as a tragedy, but as a passing to something better, something glorious.

So her mind passed over that part of the story and focused instead on Sophia. As she fell into a restful slumber, her subconscious did what it was good at—combined pieces of her

193

day together, so Sophia was wearing the purple dress that Annie had been sewing and Annie was wearing the lavender apron. When Sophia and her sister were walking through a field and Sophia dropped her blanket, it seemed fitting that Dr. Kamal stooped, picked it up, and handed it to them.

In his soft, melodic voice, he blessed both girls. "May His goodness and grace be with you both for now and evermore."

And with those words still echoing in her heart, Leah woke to the dawn's light shining through her hospital window on the day her children would be born.

21

Annie stood close to Leah's bed as both Dr. Kamal and Dr. Reese entered the room Tuesday morning. She had a good idea what they were about to say, and she'd done her best to prepare Leah without coming out and guessing they were going to deliver the babies in the next few hours. The monitors pretty much told it all. Even with the medicines pumping through Leah's IV, her blood pressure was not what Annie would have liked to see. The bigger question was, why was it remaining high?

It didn't take Dr. Reese long to move past the pleasantries and into their plan for the day.

"Your blood pressure isn't settling down as we'd like."

"Is it something I've done?"

"Not at all. More than likely the placenta is stressed, attempting to pull from the wall as your infants continue to grow. Because of this, we'd like to deliver the babies, Leah, by cesarean section."

Leah reached for Annie's hand and twined their fingers together. They'd discussed this possibility an hour before, but hearing it from her doctor, well, Annie knew hearing it would be different.

"I'd hoped it might still be possible to have a normal birth, but it seems nothing about these two *bopplin* is destined to be normal."

Dr. Kamal's smile revealed a row of perfect white teeth, as well as the fact that he was completely at ease with what lay ahead. "And this will be your first but not your last lesson that children have their own minds, yes?"

He placed his hands on her stomach as he had done so many times since Leah had arrived. "My colleague, Dr. Reese, will make her incision and lift these precious gifts out of your stomach, out of your womb. Then she will hand them over to me, Leah. You will be awake. You will hear their cry of greeting. It may sound like the mewling of a kitten rather than the bawl of a calf, if you'll excuse my animal analogies. I anticipate they will be small babies—tinier than what you are used to seeing in your community."

"How small?"

"Maybe five or six pounds. Could be more or less, but your last ultrasound indicates this range, which is good. It's a healthy weight."

"And their lungs?" Leah glanced at Annie. "You were worried about their lungs when I first arrived."

"We have given them extra time. Now they should be developed enough to breathe on their own, though I suspect we'll want to give them a little time in an incubator."

The room grew silent as all of the details sank in.

Leah's final question wasn't about the babies or about herself, it was about Adam. "Can we wait long enough for my husband to arrive?"

Dr. Reese's and Dr. Kamal's eyes met. Annie could have imagined it, but it seemed they might have discussed this earlier.

"We were hoping that four o'clock this afternoon would work for you. It seems we both have full schedules until then."

Leah closed her eyes, took in a deep breath, and nodded. "Four would be *gut*."

Annie noticed she didn't ask any questions about the actual surgery or her recovery period. Her *schweschder* had matured a lot from the young woman who was huddled on the bathroom floor two weeks ago.

The doctors had left the room, and Annie pulled up her chair. She handed Leah a cup of water, and then explained to her about the length of the incision, the type of anesthesia she would have, and what the weeks of recovery would be like. No doubt others would be in later to go over the same information, but she wanted Leah to have time to digest what was ahead.

Leah listened closely, asked a few questions, and then they prayed together for the children, the doctors, and Leah and Adam. When they finished, the clock had finally inched its way to ten o'clock.

So Annie picked up the phone, and put through the call to Samuel.

It was after lunch when there was a light tap on their door. Much too early for it to be Adam and Samuel. Leah had been attempting to nap, but without any success. Annie had been working on the quilt, an Overall Sam—purple-colored shirt, blue suspenders, blue pants, and black hat. She had thought about offering a story, a story about goodness, but Leah had seemed to prefer the quiet.

At the tap on the door, a woman peeked inside. She looked vaguely familiar, but Annie couldn't place her.

"Excuse me. I don't mean to interrupt."

"It's all right," Leah said.

The woman stepped farther into the room, and that was when Annie saw the boy behind her. There was no mistaking who he was. Her mind had travelled back to her days at Mercy too often, and then there were the letters they had exchanged regularly.

"Annie!"

Before she could store her quilting, he had hurled himself across the room and into her arms. She closed her eyes and breathed in the scent of him. There had been many patients under her care while she worked on the children's floor, but none she had grown as close to as Kiptyn.

"You have grown."

"I know. I'm not a *boppli* anymore."

He stood straight, and she was surprised to see not only that he had grown but that his color was good and he bore no resemblance at all to a cancer patient. There was no doubt about it though—he was the same boy, with the same eyes that missed nothing, and the same smile ready to pop at the smallest thing.

"This is Kiptyn?" Leah asked.

"*Ya* and his mother, Nadine."

"It's *gut* to meet you." I'm Leah, Annie's *schweschder*. Leah struggled to sit up straighter in the bed and Annie moved to hand her the controls.

"I hope this isn't a bad time." Nadine glanced from Leah to Annie and then at Kiptyn.

"*Nein.*" Leah tried to wave her left hand, but found the IV had caught in the bed rail.

"I can help you," Kiptyn said. "I had lots of IVs when I stayed here. Got real good at tangling and untangling them. Wait— you would say real *gut* at tangling and untangling them!"

He grinned as he freed the IV from where it had snagged.

"*Danki*, Kiptyn."

"*Gem gschehne*."

Annie clapped her hands. "You've remembered all the words I taught you while I was here."

"And the ones in our letters."

"How old are you, Kiptyn?" Leah asked.

"I'll be twelve soon. Mom says I'll outgrow her before I'm thirteen."

"I wouldn't be surprised. Your dad's quite tall and it seems you do take after him." Nadine smiled at her son. She reached out to touch his hair, but he ducked away.

"What's with the long hair, Kiptyn? Last time I saw you . . ." Annie rubbed her hand on the top of her *kapp*. "It was shiny up there."

Kiptyn laughed and the sound did more to heal the lonely corners of Leah's room than anything could have. His hand travelled down his head, down the hair fastened into a pony-tail in the back. "It grows fast now. I cut it once a year, and you know . . . donate it to other kids."

"Locks of Love," his mother explained. "They make hair-pieces for children who can't afford them otherwise."

"That's *wunderbaar*, Kiptyn."

"You taught me that word in our letters." Kiptyn smiled again, then focused on Leah. "You're here because of your babies?"

Leah nodded.

"Are they okay?"

"*Ya. Danki* for asking."

"My mom and dad only have me," Kiptyn said, suddenly serious. "It's the three of us, so we've vowed to look out for each other. You know?"

"I do." Leah's voice was soft and smooth. Annie could tell that she'd fallen under Kiptyn's spell. But then, who could resist? The boy had a way about him. Perhaps it was his open honesty or . . .

"We should be going." Nadine hugged her, hesitated a moment, then added, "We happened to be visiting a patient on the old floor this morning. They told us you were here. I hope it was okay to stop by."

"It was more than okay."

Kiptyn held up his hand, and rolled his eyes when she shook her head in confusion. "You're supposed to high-five it, Annie. You know. Slap it."

So she did, and it earned her an extra smile.

"I still have the wooden horse *Onkel* Eli sent me. Tell him. Will you?"

"I will."

"We'll be praying for you and your babies, Leah." Nadine put her hand to Kiptyn's back to usher him out of the room.

As he reached the door, he turned, waved good-bye, and Annie saw again the young boy she had cared for.

She sat back down, intending to resume her quilting. Instead she stared at the square she'd been sewing.

"Goodness," Leah said.

"What?"

"*Goodness* was our next gift from the scripture in Galatians, and our next story."

"*Ya* . . ."

"But this time *Gotte* sent our story. He sent Kiptyn to visit."

Adam practically jumped out of the car before it came to a stop. It was a good thing he'd been to Mercy Hospital before. He knew the way to the information desk, even if he didn't remember the way to Leah's room.

What was he thinking? She wasn't in her room. She was having their babies—right now!

The volunteers at the information desk had apparently been waiting for him. It seemed Annie had called down and alerted them he would be showing up and hurrying to make the birth. But it didn't account for the fact they knew who he was as he dashed up to the desk.

Certainly, there was more than one Amish farmer in the hospital. More than one Amish farmer, expecting children in minutes . . . or had they already arrived?

"Right this way. I'll take you to be scrubbed in."

What did that mean?

He didn't waste any time asking questions, or waiting to see if the rest of his family was behind him. They'd find their way. Leah needed him now!

Within fifteen minutes, he'd removed his coat and covered his clothes with the surgical gown. He'd also scrubbed his hands and donned a mask over his face and a cap over his hair. It would be a miracle if Leah even recognized him.

A nurse pushed open the doors to the operating room, and his senses were overwhelmed—lights, antiseptic smells, blades on a tray, the beep of countless machines. He felt the familiar nausea, like he'd experienced in Lewistown, but then he heard a voice. One he'd longed to hear, and in person, not over a phone line.

"Adam? Annie, is that Adam?"

"I think it is, though he's scoured clean and looking dapper in those green scrubs."

He saw his sister's eyes first, on the other side of a partition, and his feet carried him there. When his gaze landed on Leah, his beautiful, precious Leah, all thoughts of fainting fled.

Adam grabbed her hand and sank onto the stool that Annie rolled his way at the last second.

"Am I too late?"

"*Nein.* I knew you would make it. I told Dr. Kamal you would find a way."

"Everyone's here? Excellent." A woman, the one he had met when they'd first admitted Leah, the one he'd entrusted Leah's care to, peeked over the drape separating Leah and Adam and Annie from Leah's stomach.

"It seems we have one too many family members, but since one is a nurse, I suppose we can allow it. Are you ready, Leah?"

"*Ya.*"

"Adam?"

"Yes. *Danki* for waiting."

Dr. Reese's eyes smiled over her mask. "We didn't wait. Our last delivery ran a little longer. Seems these babies wanted their dad present."

Adam felt something surge in his heart. This was happening. Suddenly it didn't matter this birth was taking place in Philadelphia instead of in their home. He was no longer afraid of fainting. He knew he'd stay strong and remain at Leah's side. He knew, without any doubt, that God had prepared him for this moment.

"I love you, Leah."

"And I love you, Adam."

"Soon it will be four of us." His throat felt as if he'd swallowed one of his mother's large biscuits whole, and he was glad the doctor began describing what she was doing. Not that he listened to her exact words. It was background music to Annie's whispered prayers. Before it seemed possible, Dr.

Kamal was speaking. His voice calmed the hammering of Adam's heart. His voice was strong and filled with joy and certainty, like those of the men singing at a church meeting. It sounded to Adam like the voice of an angel. "We have a fine baby boy here."

Dr. Kamal held the child up, and though he was small and not yet cleaned, he was the most perfect thing Adam had ever seen. His mouth formed a large O, and then he began to cry.

"Oh, Adam—" Leah's voice was a whisper, a breath against his skin.

"Are you okay?"

"*Ya*, it's only . . . it seemed my heart stopped when I saw him."

A nurse accepted the child and carried him to a table close by.

"She'll return with him soon," Annie assured them.

Before Adam could recover from the sight of his newborn, a second howl joined the first.

"And we have another. Two sons, Adam and Leah. You have two fine sons, nearly identical in weight, though it seems the latter has more hair than the first."

Adam looked up over the drape and saw in Dr. Kamal's hand a near mirror image of the first babe, but this one had a full head of curly hair.

It was a shock for Adam, seeing their boys, seeing Amos and Ben. Yes, they had thought of names, but he hadn't pictured them, not as actual boys. By the time they'd murmured prayers of thanksgiving and shed their tears, the nurse had placed Amos on the bed next to Leah and Ben within the crook of Adam's left arm.

How could anything so small be so precious?

How could he be a father worthy of this family?

He couldn't, but he would try. With God's help he would do his best. He made the vow as Leah trailed her finger down Amos' face and ran her hand over the top of his head, which had brown fuzz instead of his brother's curls.

"We've been blessed, Adam."

"That we have. Something we'll need to remind each other of when they let the cow out of the pasture or slip out of school early on a spring afternoon."

"My boys would never do that!" Tears coursed down Leah's cheeks, even as she laughed.

"They are Adam's sons as well," Annie reminded her.

"A blessing for certain, and it will be years before such pranks."

Annie reached for Ben, and Adam carefully picked up Amos.

"For now, they are my sweet babes."

Adam couldn't argue with that. He'd been given many gifts—faith, love, and family.

He couldn't help wondering how old they'd need to be before they could ride with him behind the big workhorses. Probably best if he didn't bring that up at the moment.

22

When Annie had walked out of the surgery room and into Samuel's arms, she thought she might collapse. It wasn't from exhaustion, though she was tired. No, it was sheer relief at seeing, smelling, and being with her husband again.

Perhaps she had blocked from her mind how much she had missed him. He held her in his arms, not saying a word, but with their child pressed between them. Annie was sure she could stand there forever.

Samuel finally insisted she sit down.

Sitting now in her room at Vickie's boarding house, sitting alone, a small part of her wanted to put her head down and weep. How had she ever stood being away from home for years?

Home was where she belonged.

They had spent almost twenty-four hours together. Her mother, dad, Samuel, Adam, even Reba and Charity had managed to fit in the van Belinda had borrowed. They'd slept in shifts, walking the blocks to her room at the boarding house, bringing food back to those still in the waiting room, then switching places. Annie had been afraid to close her eyes, afraid Leah would need her or Samuel would disappear.

"You've been a *gut schweschder*," he'd whispered before he'd climbed back into the van. "And you'll be home soon."

"*Ya*. Maybe this weekend." She'd swallowed the tears threatening to spoil their parting.

Four more days. Dr. Reese and Dr. Kamal had both agreed it was possible the babies would be ready to go home Saturday. Leah was doing wonderfully well.

As the van had pulled away, a deep weariness had settled over her and she'd wondered if she'd be able to walk back into the hospital. Foster saved her when he stepped outside on his break.

"Leah's asleep, honey. She said to tell you to go get some rest."

"But—"

"No buts. You look as if you're going to drop in the street. We'll look after her, Annie. Trust us."

It was those last words—*trust us*—that had sent her home, leaving her quilting bag in Leah's room. So now she sat at the small desk, staring at her Bible, at Paul's letter to the Galatians in particular, and wondering if she would ever be able to sleep. So many thoughts were going through her mind. So many questions and worries.

Amos had needed oxygen twice today.

Ben's temperature had dipped once.

Should she have encouraged Adam to stay as he'd wanted to? But four days confined in the hospital would have seemed like an eternity with Adam pacing and trying to be helpful. At least at home he could prepare for their arrival.

She glanced down at the words in front of her, "Be guided by the Spirit . . ."

Pulling the *kapp* and pins from her head, she ran her fingers through her hair, releasing her doubts and worries as she did so. God had cared for Leah while she carried Amos and Ben.

He'd seen she was in the right place when she needed doctors around her. He'd sent kind and compassionate nurses to care for her.

"If we live by the Spirit, let's follow the Spirit." Placing her hands on her stomach, she felt her babe move, kick once, then resettle.

Foster had been right. She needed to rest. It was important to care for her child and listen to the symptoms of fatigue when they overwhelmed her—before they overwhelmed her. Marking the page in her Bible with a slip of paper, she dimmed the light and prepared for bed.

Amos had *only* needed oxygen twice today.

Ben's temperature had *only* dipped once.

The babies were growing stronger by the hour, and Leah was healing quickly.

Samuel was correct, soon they would be home.

⸙

Leah was surprised when Annie walked into her room so early the next morning. Penny had started her nursing shift and checked on her already, but the aides hadn't yet brought breakfast. As Annie pushed open the door to the room, Leah was walking from the bathroom back to her bed.

"You're up and walking early," she exclaimed.

"I'm still slow, but actually the muscles feel less sore if I move around a little every few hours."

"That's *gut*, Leah. It's what you're supposed to do, but a lot of patients resist."

"Resistance is futile, or so Foster and Penny tell me." Leah couldn't have stopped the smile spreading across her face. She realized she was going to miss the staff here at Mercy. She'd grown closer to them than she would ever have imagined. "You look rested."

"*Ya.* I did sleep well. How are my nephews?"

"Hungry. They nurse often, every three hours, but they are so precious, Annie."

"Yes, they are. You're going to need to nap in between feedings."

"No worries there." Leah sat on the bed, swinging her feet. "I pass out as soon as I'm finished feeding them. What if I do that at home? Here it's okay. There are nurses everywhere, but at home—"

"At home you'll have Adam to help. Yes, you'll both be walking around in a daze for a while, but you nap when you can. Don't worry that you won't wake when they cry. I heard both of their lungs when they were born, Leah. No mewling kittens as Dr. Kamal feared."

"More like roaring lions."

"Did I hear there were lions in this room?" Penny walked in with a tray full of food.

Leah felt her stomach growl, her stomach that was still entirely too large. "I'll never lose this baby weight if I keep eating all that you bring."

Both Annie and Penny shook their heads.

"I know. I know. Eat for the babies."

"Nursing moms do not need to worry about losing weight," Penny reminded her. "You need your strength and you need your liquids."

Annie picked up the refrain. "And we don't worry about weight, unless it's a health issue, which it's not in your case. It would be prideful to focus too much on what you weigh. You are as you should be, not to mention Adam adores you."

Leah sighed as she felt herself give in to their logic. She couldn't resist because she knew they were both right, plus the food smelled pretty good—not as good as her own cooking, but not bad. She raised the lid that covered her breakfast. "Yum. Bacon for once. Share with me, Annie?"

"Oh, no. Vickie fed me before I walked over."

———— ⚬⚬⚬ ————

Unfortunately, Leah's positive feelings didn't last. An hour later she started worrying again. What if the babies weren't able to go home on Saturday? She would probably move to Annie's room on Friday. How long could they stay at the boarding house? She didn't want to go there. She didn't want to be separated from her sons by half a mile. She didn't want to be separated at all. She needed to be close in case they needed her. They would need her. They nursed every three hours!

"You're frowning again," Annie said, pulling her needle and thread through another of the Dutch boy squares.

"*Ya.* I know."

"Worrying?"

"I suppose."

She appreciated the fact Annie didn't try to talk her out of it, and she didn't even attempt to list all the things she was fretting over—they were so obvious. Not to mention she was tired of sitting in the bed, tired of this room, and when she'd sneezed earlier she was sure her incision had ripped open. It hadn't. Annie had helped her check.

This day felt like it would never end.

"Now your frown looks like *dat's* when he's unhappy about the weather."

"I've never seen your *dat* frown."

"Do you remember the drought before I left on my *rumspringa*?"

"I was young."

"*Ya*, definitely not engaged to Adam yet. The drought didn't last long, but it was extreme enough to threaten that year's crops. Oh, how *dat* would pace and frown, as if he could bring rain from the sky. I can still remember *mamm* telling him to trust in *Gotte's* faithfulness. *Dat* would stare at her, then traipse back out to the barn."

Leah shook her head. "You're making that up."

"I'm not. We children made ourselves scarce that year. Things were tense in the house."

Silence filled the room as Annie continued to sew, and Leah pictured Rebekah and Jacob. She'd spoken to her own family once since Amos and Ben were born—they'd called from a phone shack near their home. She'd promised to write regularly about both boys' progress. Rebekah and Jacob had traveled in the van though, and slept in the chairs in the waiting room. They were precious to her.

"How did it end?" Leah asked.

"With rain, as droughts always end."

Leah sighed. "There's so much to worry about, Annie. I didn't know being a *mamm* would include so much . . . well, so much fear!"

Annie completed the stitching around the Dutch boy's bright blue shirt and dark blue pants. "I suppose there is, but *Gotte* is always faithful. *Ya?*"

A smile tugged at the corner of Leah's lips, in spite of her determination to hold on to her pout. "I suppose."

"He was faithful when he brought me home to Mifflin County."

Leah stared out the window. A light snow covered the tall buildings and even the tiny parked cars below. "He was faithful when He brought me and Adam together at the singing after church when I was seventeen. I rarely went to singings."

Annie laughed. "Adam never went to singings. He sings like an old bull."

Someone passed in the hall. The soft shoes squeaked on the linoleum floor, echoing until the sound faded away. "He was faithful when He gave me two sons. There are some women in our community who have none."

Annie nodded. "*Ya*, and I know that *Gotte* fills their home too—with nieces and nephews . . ."

"And there is that one family in the other district who adopted children from the city. *Gotte* is faithful, Annie." Leah's fears ebbed away as she realized the truth of their testimony.

"He is that."

"Our list could go on for a very long time." She snuggled down into her bed.

"Yes, it could."

"But I believe I'll rest now. Our list is a *gut* story for your Dutch boy—for the fruit of faithfulness."

"It's an excellent story." Annie stood and closed the blinds so the light that came into the room was somewhat softer. The last thing Leah saw before sleep claimed her was the snow beginning to fall again. Her last thought was to wonder if it was also falling at home.

23

Adam stood with his hands in his pockets, frowning at Dr. Kamal. "But we agreed that today the boys would come home. I've waited all day, and Belinda—she brought the van. Everything is ready."

Dr. Kamal nodded in agreement. "Yes, I see why you are upset. However, babies, they do not always follow the plans we lay out for them. Isn't this true?"

Adam glanced around the crowded room. Leah, Annie, Belinda, and Dr. Kamal all stared back at him. No one seemed to know what to say. They'd been waiting all day long for Dr. Kamal to return. Now darkness was covering the city, and Adam had hoped they would be on their way.

The boys had been in the room, but a man close to Adam's age, Foster was the name written on his name tag, had taken the boys out after they'd fallen asleep. Adam couldn't believe how they'd grown in less than a week. He couldn't believe they needed to spend another night in Philadelphia.

Dr. Kamal studied his shoes a moment longer; when he finally did speak, he held his hands out in front of him. They were large hands—Adam thought they looked like a farmer's hands. Dark black on the outside, pink on his palms, they were hands that had helped bring his sons into this world.

Because of that, Adam pushed down his impatience and listened.

"In my country, especially in the villages, these babies would be home already. Here in America we are more careful. Are we too careful?" He shrugged. "We've found there are four things that are important to see before a baby goes home, especially the small ones like Amos and Ben."

Adam liked that the doctor remembered his sons' names. He seemed to be a kind man, and no doubt he was doing what he thought was best.

"First of all, they need to breathe without the use of oxygen."

"Amos has not needed the oxygen since Thursday," Leah pointed out.

Adam recognized the strain in her voice, and he moved closer to her bed. He'd vowed to be there for her emotionally. Reaching out, he placed his hand through the raised bar of the bed, covered her hand, and squeezed.

"It's true. Neither boy has needed respiratory support." Kamal ticked off one finger. "We also watch their heart rates and breathing patterns. The twins were nearly thirty-six weeks and had no problem with either of these things."

He ticked another finger, looked up, and winked at Annie.

"The third thing we need to see is if they take all their feedings by mouth."

"How else—" Adam glanced over at Belinda.

"Some babies need a feeding tube," she answered. "We couldn't do that in your home."

"Amos and Ben are doing well. They lost a little weight at first, which is normal, and have begun to gain again. I'm very happy to see this." The smile on Dr. Kamal's face was genuine and did much to ease the knot in Adam's stomach. Releasing the boys to go home would have done a lot more.

"Our problem is in the fourth area—maintaining a stable temperature. Amos has managed to do this. It is Ben whose temperature dipped a small amount in the wee hours this morning. It was not much and not for long, but I like to see an acceptable, stable temperature for twenty-four hours before I release an infant to go home—"

Adam began to interrupt him, but the good doctor pushed on.

"And I'm aware while Amish homes are comfortably heated for adults with your wood stoves, it might not provide the level of warmth a premature infant with temperature instability would need."

Adam was shocked. "You know how we heat our homes?"

Dr. Kamal shrugged. "It's my job to know about my patients, Adam. Also, we are in Philadelphia, not New Guinea. You're not my first Amish parent."

Adam stared down at the floor, thinking and praying. When he looked up, he asked, "If we weren't Amish, would you send him home?"

"No! Not until twenty-four hours have passed. Maybe tomorrow. With the promise that you will find a way to maintain a steady temperature in the babes' room of—"

"*Ya.* Annie already told us. The bishop has approved the use of a generator and it's all in place. We have the extra heaters, if need be. I assure you, the workmanship on my house is *gut.* I'll put it up beside your fancy city dwelling any day."

Dr. Kamal nodded as if he expected as much. "Then we will hope for tomorrow, and I will make my rounds early."

<hr />

Belinda and Annie had gone to sleep at the boarding house. Adam was moving things around so that he could sleep in the chair which stretched out into a bed, when Leah began giggling.

"What do you find funny, *fraa*?"

"You won't fit in that chair as easily as Annie did."

"I won't?"

"*Nein*. Your legs will hang off the end, and you're going to have to sleep on your side to fit at all." Then her voice grew wistful. "I wish you could sleep here with me."

Adam glanced around the room, shrugged, and began to drag the chair over next to her bed.

"You're going to rearrange their furniture?"

"Why not? I've missed you, Leah."

"And I've missed you."

"At least we can sleep side by side." He finished positioning the chair, then noticed Annie's quilt draped across the arm. "Are you two still working on this?"

"*Ya*. It's taken a little longer than we thought it would."

Adam held it out in front of him. They'd only left one light on in the room as they'd prepared for bed, but he could make out the pattern. Leah and Annie had always been good quilters, but he didn't see anything particularly hard about this design, certainly nothing that should have caused them trouble.

"I guess you didn't have as much free time as you thought you would."

"Oh we had a lot of time, but we kept stopping to tell stories."

"Stories?" Adam unfolded the sheet the nurse had given him to cover up with. "What kind of stories?"

Leah reached for the quilt. "A story for each child. It started when I first came here, before I apologized to you about my behavior—"

"No need to speak of that again. We're past those days. Forgotten and forgiven."

"*Ya*, but I mention it because Annie had been reading the Bible, and she read Galatians five, verse twenty-two."

"I should remember what that is. I know Paul wrote it."

As Adam stretched out on the chair and deep night settled around them, Leah told him the stories from the quilt and how they matched up with the fruits of the Spirit.

"All we have left is the boy she finished yesterday and the heart, here in the middle at the bottom. She decided to add it to make the quilt different. To make it special."

"So you've done seven of the nine fruits. The two you have left would be—"

"Gentleness"—Leah's voice was a whisper—"and self-control."

"The final two fruits of the Spirit."

"*Ya*."

Adam had never been one to read stories very much—Annie did that. He read *The Budget*, and occasionally he'd read a mechanics magazine he saw at the library. He read the Bible, more now than ever before, though he couldn't say he understood everything he read. Maybe with each year that passed, he would understand more.

Curling up on the chair in the hospital room, staring into his wife's beautiful eyes, he searched his heart, and he found the story she needed to hear. It was a story about a man, who had been a boy. He had spent nearly three weeks alone while his wife and unborn children had been at the hospital. During that time he had learned a lot about himself, about self-control, and about love and the importance of treating one another with gentleness. He touched the heart on the quilt when he came to that part.

He wasn't sure his story was very good, but his wife had tears in her eyes and a smile on her lips, so he supposed it was good enough. They fell asleep holding hands, and they were awakened two hours later by the sound of two crying, hungry little boys. Adam was groggy, and he felt like someone had rubbed dirt in his eyes. Something told him that before the year was out he'd be used to their new routine—and besides, all things passed.

Leah walked through her home slowly, touching each item as if she'd never seen it before. She remembered the day they'd married, the first night she'd spent there with Adam. Even those memories couldn't compare to this evening.

"The bassinets are in our room—one on each side of the bed." Adam joined her in the sitting room, looking quite pleased with himself. "And I'd say this house is toasty warm."

"*Ya*. Dr. Kamal should come visit and see for himself." Leah couldn't believe that just the night before they'd been worried they wouldn't get to come home. Twenty-four hours could change so much. "Do you think we should have let Annie stay?"

"*Nein*. We can handle the *bopplin*. I'll help you, Leah. And if I know my *mamm*, she'll be here in the morning."

"It was *gut* of her to leave the food."

"They'll all bring food. You won't need to worry about cooking until the boys are sleeping at least six hours straight."

Leah sat on their couch, then ran her hand over the arm. How long since she had sat on a couch? It had been hospital beds and hospital chairs for weeks. Then she closed her eyes and listened.

"Sleeping?" Adam's voice was very close to her ear.

Goosebumps popped out down her neck and along her arms as he sat down next to her.

"I was listening."

"*Ya?*"

"Listening to the silence. It's beautiful."

"I like it."

"Mercy was a *gut* place, but it always had sounds. This is better."

"It's better now that you're here—you and Amos and Ben."

The wind rattled the window, but the house remained snug and warm.

"Do you know what I think we should do, Leah?" Adam's voice teased her ear again.

She shook her head. When she looked into his eyes, she saw the old Adam, with the mischievous grin.

"Help ourselves to the plate of oatmeal raisin cookies *mamm* left, with some cold milk."

"It's so late—"

"All the better. Before the boys wake up. Makes me hungry getting up so often during the night."

"You've done it once!"

"Exactly. I know what it's like, so I'm fortifying myself." He made his way to the kitchen. She listened to him pull out glasses from the cabinet, open the refrigerator, pour milk, and bring everything into the living room.

She was home.

The word resounded through her heart.

And it was as sweet as the fresh-baked cookie Adam offered.

24

Annie sat in her sewing room on Christmas Eve, grateful she had a few free hours to put the binding around Leah's quilt. How had the weeks slipped away? It seemed yesterday they were walking down the streets of town, looking in the windows, and planning for Thanksgiving.

That holiday had come and gone and now another was upon them. Life would slip by like leaves in the wind if she wasn't careful. Her mother had warned her. "Don't blink, Annie. Don't get caught up in worrying over the little things. You'll miss the daily blessings *Gotte* has in store for you."

The baby kicked, as if agreeing with her mother's words of wisdom. Would she ever take anything for granted again? After being away from her home for so long? After being through such a time with Leah?

And yet it had been a blessing. She'd known it the moment Adam had walked into the hospital room. The second his eyes had landed on his wife. Her brother had changed in those weeks. Much as Leah had matured in Philadelphia, Adam had learned to cherish and adore what mattered the most in his life—a young woman and two precious children.

"You're concentrating awfully hard in here."

Annie turned in her chair. Samuel was leaning against the doorframe, watching her. He stood with his arms crossed, and she could see his hands were clean so he must have been inside for a while. She'd never heard him come in from the barn!

"I suppose I am," she admitted.

"Anything you'd like to share?"

Annie sighed and continued stitching the binding to the quilting. It lay nicely, attaching the back of the quilt against the front. It provided an edge around the rows of Dutch children, safely tucking them together, binding them together.

"I told you about our stories? The ones we told while we waited through the days and nights? The ones that went with the children?"

"*Ya.* The stories matched the fruits of the Spirit. That was a *gut* idea. It helped you both to focus on the blessings *Gotte* had in store rather than worry." Samuel walked into the room and sat down across from her. "Smart thinking, Annie."

Shaking her head, Annie continued stitching the last row of binding, finishing what she had started so long ago, what she had intended to complete before Amos and Ben were born. "It wasn't my idea though. It was Leah's. Maybe *Gotte* whispered the idea to her. *Ya?*"

"Maybe so." Samuel's voice was quiet and gentle, as it usually was.

"Do you think stories can serve a purpose?"

Samuel took his time answering. He waited until she had finished the last of the row, tied off her thread, and clipped it. "I believe anything can serve *Gotte's* purpose. We know as much from the Word—whether it be an unwilling prophet, or a donkey, a whale, loaves and fishes . . ."

"A quilt," Annie whispered. "Or an infant."

"Indeed."

The babe within her moved again, poking an elbow or foot out. Annie reached for Samuel's hand, placed it over her stomach. "I believe she has your feet!"

Instead of laughing, he took the quilt from her hands, placed it on the table, and then pulled her into his lap.

"I'm too big."

"You're not."

"I am. I've gained three pounds this month."

"And I'm glad."

Annie laughed and wrapped her arms around his neck, burrowing into his embrace.

"I missed you." When the tears began to fall, she didn't try to explain them, didn't attempt to stop them, but rather allowed herself a moment of complete openness.

Instead of questioning her, Samuel unpinned her *kapp*, placed it beside the quilt and ran his fingers through her hair, loosening the curls. It seemed to Annie, as he brushed out her braid with his fingers, he also brushed away the last of the tension—the final fragments of worry she'd held inside. For a moment, she could rest and allow Samuel to care for her.

She must have fallen asleep, because she woke later in her bed, the smell of dinner coming up the stairs.

It was a simple meal. She'd started the stew earlier in the day, and Samuel had baked cornbread to go with it. Not fancy at all, but that dinner did more to heal her heart than a feast could have. Though they'd been back for two weeks, the evening healed the bruised places from her time away. A part of her mind realized she was exhausted and she'd be better very soon. Another part kept turning over the idea this was their last Christmas Eve alone. Next year it would be three at their table, and God willing, perhaps more in coming years.

For this evening, with the candlelight in the window, her husband sitting across from her, and Leah's finished quilt upstairs, ready to give, Annie knew the peace of Christmas.

⸺∞⸺

Leah sat in her living room, uncomfortable that she wasn't helping clean up the dishes from their holiday meal—the meal they shared on Second Christmas, the day after the official Christmas celebration. Yesterday she and Adam had spent alone, reading the Scripture and enjoying the holiness of the day with their boys. Today was a day for family and for the giving of gifts.

Then Ben began fussing and Jacob quickly handed him over. "I believe he wants you, *mamm*. Maybe it's time to eat?"

"*Nein*. Rocking him will settle him down. His *dat* has spoiled him already."

"Guilty," Adam agreed from the checkerboard, where he was apparently losing to Zeke.

"He'll be free to rock the baby in a minute, Leah. He's about to be beaten again."

Leah didn't hear what Adam said in reply, but Zeke's laughter was all she needed. It did her heart a good turn to see genuine smiles on the faces of Rachel's boys. And was *Onkel* Eli the one to thank for that? She couldn't be sure, but it would seem, from the attentiveness he paid to Rachel, possibly an announcement would be coming soon. Theirs wouldn't be the first wedding plans to occur in this family around Christmas.

"Such a small one," Jacob was saying. "I believe I've caught bigger fish."

"*Dat*—" Charity's voice rose in warning, but Leah quickly reassured them both.

"Adam says the same. Though both boys are now well over six pounds."

"Six! It's a miracle. That's what it is." Rebekah wiped her hands on a dish towel as she ushered Annie, Reba, and Rachel into the living room.

How they'd managed to bring the Christmas meal to Leah and Adam's house, plus serve it there when they barely had enough dishes for the two of them, Leah didn't know. But they'd done it, and she was grateful. She hadn't wanted to take Amos and Ben out in the snow, even if it was only a dusting and there was little wind. Doctor Kamal, Samuel, and Annie had all thought indoors was best for the first month, though having family in the room was fine as long as no one was sick.

Leah looked around and realized that though she missed her parents, brothers, and sisters in Wisconsin, this was her family now, and they meant everything to her. They'd support her, Adam, and the boys through the months and years ahead.

Adam's gaze met hers, a smile playing on his lips. He did that a lot lately. It was as if he was looking for chances to show how much he cared. It caught her off guard sometimes. It reminded her of when they were courting, and she found herself taking extra time when she combed her hair or dressed in the morning. Now she found herself resting during the day so that she could have the energy to stay up and talk with Adam in the evening. Those moments with her husband were precious, and she was determined to guard them.

"I believe it's gift-giving time," Jacob said, standing and using his cane for support.

He looked slowly around the room, his eyes lingering on each one. Their numbers had grown this year, not only because of the two additional babes, but Trent was also included. He'd agreed to the terms set by the bishop. The year ahead would be difficult, but they would all pray for him and encourage him. If he made it through the adjustment period of leaving behind the technological advances he'd need to give up, then he and Reba could marry the following October.

David was also there with Charity, which surprised no one. Perhaps the fall would include another double wedding—or even three if the things she'd heard about Rachel and Eli were true. From the way Rachel had softened, it seemed love could pass your way, even after you'd travelled quite a long distance down life's road.

Jacob cleared his throat and continued. "Let us not forget, as we give these gifts of love, the reason we give. On this day, so many years ago, *Gotte* shared His grace with each of us in Christ Jesus. This is why we celebrate."

Leah noticed a smile pass around the room between each person, like bread passed on a platter. Jacob never preached, but he always reminded. His was a kind and gentle guidance.

"We are especially thankful this day for the gift of Amos and Ben. Each of you are responsible for praying for these precious *kinner*, and also for helping raise them, for children need an entire family, not merely a *mamm* and *dat*. They need *onkels* and *aentis* and cousins as well."

There was some laughter now as each person began whispering plans. Leah heard some of them, plans to teach her boys to fish or to ride a pony. She closed her eyes and heard their words, blessings upon her children, and they were better than any material gifts that might be given.

Jacob held up his hands. "We will add at least one other before we meet for this Christmas celebration again."

Samuel stood behind Annie. He leaned forward and whispered something in her ear.

"Perhaps more." Jacob's expression turned serious as he looked first toward Trent, then David, and finally Rachel. It would seem he knew well what was going on within his family. "Remember, pray for one another. We accept and believe prayers are mighty and powerful things. They are indeed."

Silence filled the room. Leah stared down into Ben's face, perfectly formed, curly hair softly covering his head, and somber eyes that gazed at her with such trust. It was his brother, Amos, who broke the solemn moment with a rather loud burp.

"Excuse us," Adam said with a laugh.

"You are excused." Jacob grinned. "And now for the gifts."

Like Leah's own family, the giving was simple, for each person had drawn a name the year before. Her sons, though, received small items from everyone there, and she found her heart filling with such gratitude that tears threatened once more. When Annie slipped her gift on top of the pile, Leah handed her Amos, and reached for the quilt.

"You finished it!"

"*Ya*. Added the binding and label on Christmas Eve."

"It's beautiful, Annie."

They both stared down at the five Dutch boys, three girls, and the single heart—the nine gifts of the Spirit. Realizing it was futile to try to put all she was feeling into words, she stood and embraced her best friend.

"I love you."

"And I you. Now, I'll go place this on the crib while you open Adam's gift."

Leah turned to her husband in surprise. They had no money for gift giving. She'd knitted him a scarf before she'd left for the hospital in Lewistown, but how had he . . .

"All those nights I was alone, I needed, that is to say, I wanted something to do." Adam sat beside her. "This was a way to put all my missing you into something constructive."

Leah accepted the large shopping bag and removed the tissue paper. Inside was a beautifully made flower box and three packages of seeds.

"We'll put it outside—"

"The bedroom window. I asked you long ago."

"And I said there was no time to make such frivolous things, or to stand and watch the birds and butterflies that would come to it." Adam ran his thumb over the back of her hand and it seemed for a moment it was only the two of them in the middle of their living room even though it was full of people. "I'd like to ask your forgiveness for that now."

"You don't—"

"But I do. I was wrong about that, as well as a few other things. It only takes a few minutes to look out a window, Leah. To appreciate what *Gotte* has given. It's important to do so, and I thank you for teaching me as much."

She didn't realize she was crying until he reached forward and brushed away her tears.

From somewhere across the room Ben let out a howl, followed by laughter from their guests.

"My son has healthy lungs, *ya*?"

"He does, Adam."

Though the boys still had a little ways to go and would need to be watched closely for a few months, it was the best Christmas Leah ever had. When they'd cleaned up and everyone had left, she stood in the doorway, Adam's arm around her waist, watching them drive away.

It was amazing she didn't feel even a little lonely. She felt as if she'd been covered in love. As they walked back into their living room, into their cozy small house with their two infant sons, she understood they'd make it through the next six months and the years after as well. They'd probably need to depend on their friends and family at some point. They'd certainly need to depend on their faith, on their God. And they'd learned they could depend on each other.

It was as if she'd stepped into a dream and wakened to find it was her life. Perhaps not all perfect, certainly not all happiness and roses, but all as God intended. Which was enough to bring peace to her heart.

Epilogue

Late March

Annie was grateful Samuel stayed near her side. Though she'd been through many births in the last several years, and certainly Leah's had been the most traumatic, she was finding none of those compared to her own. Watching was one thing. Helping another. Giving birth herself? A different thing entirely.

Samuel counted softly in her ear, in German, and she panted her breath out in rapid beats. Her world was Samuel, the child in her womb, and their room, which had become a sanctuary.

"I believe we're ready, Annie."

She focused on Belinda's directions from the foot of the bed, clutched Samuel's hand, and concentrated on the strength and love of the man at her side. She couldn't have said if twenty minutes passed or an hour. There was daylight peeping through her bedroom curtains, and Belinda's and Samuel's caring hands on her skin.

Then the pain ended as abruptly as it had begun. The midwife was laughing as she asked, "And what did you say you'd be naming the child?"

"Bethany." Samuel's voice was solid and sure, and his kisses were as welcome as the cool rag he pressed to her face. "We've decided to call her Bethany, which means '*Gotte's* disciple.'"

"I know what the name means, Samuel. You'll have to be saving it though. Today you will need a name for a boy."

"*Nein.*"

"*Ya.* See for yourself." Belinda set the infant on Annie's stomach and handed Samuel the scissors.

At that moment, Annie thought her heart might burst. Somehow, she managed to whisper, "Cut the cord quickly, Samuel."

Seeing her child, after all those months of feeling him moving inside her, she suddenly could not wait even one moment longer to hold him.

"*Ya*, I'll hurry." Samuel's voice was husky as Belinda clamped and he cut the cord that had bound their son to her, severing the lifeline that had provided his sustenance.

Then Rebekah was there, wiping him clean, performing the APGAR test, and wrapping him first in a warm blanket and then in a quilt, one sewn by her hands and no doubt prayed over for many hours.

"We didn't even think of a boy's name," Annie whispered.

"The Lord brought us together through your father, Annie. It would seem fitting . . ."

They both stared down at the child her mother had placed in the crook of her arm. His head was covered with brown curly hair, more than it seemed an infant could have.

"Jacob, we love you." Annie kissed him at the same moment her husband kissed her. Laughter echoed in the hall as Rebekah shared the news.

Annie's eyes were incredibly heavy, and she struggled to keep them open after her long night of hard labor. She thought of Leah's quilt and the nine fruits—love, joy, peace, patience, kindness, goodness, faithfulness, gentleness, and self-control. Her mind leafed through the nine stories of the nine precious children, like so many pages in a book—except this book was the story of their life.

Now between them they'd received the gift of three boys who would grow up together in God's grace.

The promise of the Spirit's fruits, the gift of life, and the certainty of God's grace.

Her last thought before falling into a restful sleep was that she had received more than a sixteen-year-old girl, driving away from Mifflin County on her *rumspringa*, could have ever dreamed.

Glossary

Aenti—aunt
Boppli—baby
Bopplin—babies
Bruder—brother
Dat—father
Danki—thank you
Englischer—non-Amish person
Fraa—wife
Freinden—friends
Gem gschehne—you're welcome
Gotte—God
Gotte's wille—God's will
Grandkinner—grandchildren
Gudemariye—good morning
Gut—good
In lieb—in love
Kaffi—coffee
Kapp—prayer covering
Kind—child
Kinner—children
Mamm—mom

Narrisch—crazy
Nein—no
Onkel—uncle
Rumspringa—running around; time before an Amish young person has officially joined the church, which provides a bridge between childhood and adulthood.
Schweschder—sister
Was iss letz—what's wrong
Wunderbaar—wonderful
Ya—yes

Discussion Questions

1. We learn in the first few pages Annie and Leah are expecting their first children. Annie's pregnancy is going smoothly. Leah seems to be having more trouble—physically and emotionally. Why do you think this is? Does God love Leah less, or is there another reason people face tough times?

2. Annie and Samuel help Mattie and Jesse when he is having a heart attack. Later Annie speaks to Samuel about the agony Mattie was going through while Jesse was hurting. Go back to chapter four and read Samuel's reply. He compares two hearts to two vines growing side by side. Is this a good analogy, and if so, why?

3. In chapter six, Jacob says, "When a thing is broken inside a person, way down deep inside, it can become infected. It can affect everything else—like the infection in my leg affected my entire body. Like the dirt in the engines you fix affect the entire machine. Until the person allows the Lord to see their deepest needs, their deepest fears, they're likely to limp along." What sorts of things do we try to hide, from others and the Lord? How does this hinder our health both spiritually and physically?

4. In chapter nine, Annie first hears Leah is in labor. She's worried about early delivery and what the babies will weigh. Samuel's response calms her. He reminds her of God's sovereignty and God's care. When have you needed to be reminded of this?

5. In chapter twelve, Leah wakes in a different room, a different hospital, completely disoriented. Though she doesn't understand all that has happened, she begins to pray, and she begins with a prayer of thanksgiving. How can prayer help steady us emotionally and physically?

6. In chapter fourteen, Adam and Leah share Habakkuk 3:19—not a book from the Bible that we read often, but it is what Adam found to ease her worries. What portions of the Bible have been a comfort to you in times of trial?

7. We see the benefit auction, through Adam's eyes, in chapter eighteen. Amish are famous for such auctions and for helping one another. What types of things occur in your community to assist others in need?

8. In chapter twenty-one we meet Kiptyn, one of Annie's previous patients. When asked, he explains that he grows his hair long for Locks of Love. Do you have any experience with this organization or other organizations that help children in need?

9. Samuel says, "I believe anything can serve *Gotte's* purpose." Do you agree? What things have you seen used by God recently?

10. The fruits of the Spirit was a major theme in this book— love (Bethany), joy (Josiah), peace (Nailah), patience (Adam), kindness (Sophia), goodness (Kiptyn), faithfulness (list of God's faithfulness), gentleness, and self-control (Adam). Reread Paul's list in Galatians, chapter five, then discuss how those gifts are an important part of our Christian witness.

Want to learn more about author
Vannetta Chapman and check out other great
fiction by Abingdon Press?

Sign up for our fiction newsletter at
www.AbingdonPress.com
to read interviews with your favorite authors, find tips
for starting a reading group, and stay posted on
what's new on the horizon. It's a place to connect
with other fiction readers or post a
comment about this book.

Be sure to visit Vannetta online!

http://www.vannettachapman.com
http://vannettachapman.wordpress.com

We hope you enjoyed Vannetta Chapman's *A Christmas Quilt* and that you will continue to read the Quilts of Love series of books from Abingdon Press.

Here's an excerpt from the next book in the series, *Aloha Rose*, by Lisa Carter.

∽∾∽

1

"Are you sure there's no message waiting for Laney Carrigan?"

Laney leaned over the information desk at the Kailua-Kona Airport. "I was supposed to be met here . . ." She gestured around the rapidly emptying lobby. "By my Auntie Teah. Maybe she's been delayed and she left a note for me with instructions?"

The airport employee, a willowy blond, craned her head around Laney at the line of people queuing behind her. She pointed down the corridor. "You can rent a car over that way." She raised her gaze above Laney's five-foot-three-inch height. "Who's next?"

Laney tightened her lips. Dismissed. Again.

"Maybe an intercom page directing me to meet someone in Baggage Claim or Ground Transportation . . .?" Laney sighed at the bored face of the woman and stepped aside as a middle-aged man wearing a flamingo pink aloha shirt shouldered past her to the front of the line. Grabbing the handle of her wheeled carry-on bag, she skirted past a group of Asian tourists who'd been greeted by hula girls bearing fragrant yellow leis.

No point in trying to rent a car when she had no idea where she was going. She paused in an out-of-the-way corner and fumbled in a side pocket of her luggage for her cell phone. Pressing the phone to ON, she waited for it to come to life.

Auntie Teah, whom she'd yet to meet, had assured her over the course of several phone calls that she would be here to welcome her long-lost niece to her ancestral home. An ancestral home to which she'd not been given directions or an address.

Hitting the Rodrigues phone number she'd stored in her cell, she tapped her navy blue stiletto-clad foot on the shiny, white airport floor and waited for someone to pick up. And waited. After ringing four times, voice mail—a deep, rumbling man's voice—informed her that no one was currently at home—duh—and instructed callers to leave a callback number at the tone. Laney snorted, not trusting herself to speak, thumbed the phone to OFF, and stuffed it into her bag. She stalked down the passageway toward Baggage Claim.

Some welcome.

Laney pushed her shoulders back, trying to ease the tension of her muscles. As her brigadier father never failed to point out, when stressed, she hunched down like Quasimodo. And with her diminutive stature, there was no one Laney wanted to resemble less than that hunchback of literary legend. She scanned the dwindling crowd encircling the baggage carousel.

Where was her Auntie Teah? Her cousin, Elyse, or Elyse's sweet little boy, Daniel? They'd promised to be here. Laney glanced at her black leather sports watch, noted the time in addition to the barometric pressure and altimeter reading. Her own barometric pressure rising, Laney shoved her bag to the ground, threw herself on top, and faced the doorway. Nobody had ever dared ignore Brigadier General Thomas Carrigan.

Apparently, his daughter, not so much.

She'd told her dad this was a bad idea, but he'd insisted she answer the inquiry in response to the information he'd posted regarding the scant facts they knew of her birth twenty-eight years ago. The website, which specialized in reuniting adoptive children with their biological families, had been silent for months. And Laney was fine with that.

Abso-flipping, positutely fine with that.

Really.

She'd never been curious as to her biological family. She'd always known her real parents, Gisela and Tom Carrigan, adopted her when she was a few months old. They'd chosen her—as her mother had often reminded her. Loved, cherished, protected her. But Gisela succumbed to a lingering, painful death to cancer three years ago.

Then her dad—administrative guru to the five stars at the Pentagon, able to cut through bureaucratic red tape and leap over snafus in a single bound—had the bright idea to post a picture of the quilt in which she'd come wrapped on their apartment doorstep.

And voilá, a hit less than twenty-four hours later.

He did some checking—to make sure none of them were serial killers—and declared it would be good for Laney to plan a visit to their home on the Big Island. Good to connect with people who knew something about her family background. Good to fulfill her adopted mother's last wish that she one day reunite with her biological family.

Laney swallowed a sob. She'd believed she'd already found her forever family. She glanced around the claim area. Her lower lip trembled at the sight of a suitcase going round and round the carousel.

Unclaimed. Alone. Like her.

She squared her shoulders. Who needed these people? The ones who'd abandoned her, deserted her. Left her behind.

Laney closed her eyes on the hateful, treacherous tears that threatened to spill out from beneath her lashes and wondered how soon she could book a return flight to D.C.

This had been a very bad idea.

"I don't get why I have to be the one to go get this woman, Mama Teah. Why can't Elyse—?" Kai held the phone a few inches away from his ear.

When the roar on the other end subsided, he cradled it once again between his head and his neck as he negotiated a curve around the lava-strewn rubble dotting the mountain side of the highway leading toward the airport, a now dormant volcano's last little hiccup some two hundred years ago. He gripped the wheel of his truck and glanced to his right at the cerulean hues of the Pacific.

"Okay, okay. I get that Elyse was called in to work and Ben's on Daniel duty, but I just stepped off the helipad and I didn't get your message until a few minutes ago." Kai frowned. "I'm on my way." He peered at the clock on the dashboard. "ETA in ten. But what aren't you telling me, Teah? Has something happened to you?" His voice caught. "Or to Tutu Mily?"

A pause on the other end.

"Teah? Where are you? You're scaring—" Kai banged his hand on the steering wheel. "I knew something like this was going to happen. I told you this was a bad idea to bring in an outsider at a time like this. I—"

"Kai Alexander Barnes." Teah's voice trumpeted in the truck cab.

Never a good sign when your foster mother used your full, legal name.

Kai winced as Teah told him in no uncertain terms what she thought of his thoughts on her ideas. "But surely, there's another way, Teah. We take care of our own. We don't need some overprivileged East Coast socialite barging into our business. Family takes care of family. Like you and Daddy Pete took care of me." His chin wobbled.

A sigh on Teah's end. "You're family in every way that counts, Kai." Her tone toughened. "Laney Carrigan is family, too."

Kai made a right turn into the airport parking lot, willing himself not to relent. This woman—and you'd better believe he'd Googled her—was as elusive as an ice cube in a lava flow. Even with his connections, he'd not been able to blast through the security firewalls her prominent army dad raised for her protection over the years. Not a single photograph to his knowledge existed of the mysterious Ms. Carrigan.

He snorted. "Anyone can post a picture of a quilt. We don't know if that quilt is really hers or how it came into her possession. We don't know if that quilt is the quilt Tutu Mily made years ago for her unborn grandbaby before Mily's daughter ran off to—"

"Bring her to the house as soon as you can," Teah interjected. "I've prayed about this, Kai. Didn't know what to do to solve our dilemma and more importantly, with Tutu's condition worsening, I'm hoping this will bring Mily some peace. I'm still praying. But I believe God's going to work this out."

Kai heard the smile in her voice over the wireless.

Teah continued. "How else do you explain after all these years of wondering when Elyse met a tourist at the resort who mentioned how he'd found his biological parents through that website and then just one day later when Elyse logged into the site, Tutu's quilt appeared?"

He ground his teeth. "I'm parking now, Teah. I promise to deliver Ms. Carrigan safe and sound to your doorstep ASAP."

"You be sure you do that, son." Teah clicked off.

Kai stared at the phone in his hand. The dial tone echoed in the truck cab. Nabbing an empty space, he pulled to a stop and put the F150 in Park. Killing the engine, the door dinged as he thrust it open, swinging his boot-clad feet to the pavement.

She'd made up her mind. And when Teah Rodrigues got something in the bit of her teeth, she was worse than any stallion on the ranch. Unstoppable. Unquenchable. Unswerving.

A force of nature. A regular Typhoon Teah. And like a silent, offshore earthquake, the aftershocks of this unknown family prodigal—Laney Carrigan—returning to the fold might prove to be their undoing.

His face hardened. Just let her try.

No way, no how, he'd let some *haole* bimbo take advantage of his family. Not on his watch.

⚬⚬⚬

Feeling the whoosh of air over her closed eyelids and the sound of the glass doors of the terminal sliding open, Laney opened her eyes. A Caucasian man stepped through and stopped, his polarized sunglasses obscuring his eyes. As the doors swished shut behind him, Laney took in his appearance—the khaki cargo pants, the ocean blue polo shirt that stretched taut across broad shoulders, the rugged jawline in need of a shave. He searched the room for someone.

Lest he catch her staring, she dropped her eyes to the floor and noticed his scuffed boots.

Tall, dark, and cowboy.

Definitely not Auntie Teah or Elyse. Whoever he was looking for, it wouldn't be her. He wasn't here for her.

242

Guys like him never were.

Cowboy pushed his glasses onto the crown of his close-cropped dark hair revealing eyes as tropical blue as the waters off the Seychelles, her last assignment. His head rotated from side to side, scrutinizing the remaining occupants of the baggage claim area. His eyes eventually came round to her. With the intensity of an electric blue flash.

Resisting the urge to fan herself—was it just her or had the temp risen another notch?—she pushed her glasses farther up the bridge of her nose and sat primly atop her carry-on case. His eyes traveled over her from the top of her head to her best-interview pointy-toed shoes. Self-conscious, she tucked her feet under her body, smoothing the edges of her pleated navy skirt over her ankles. Cowboy's eyes narrowed before flicking away at the sound of a voice down the corridor, dismissing her as she knew he would.

"Kai! Wait up!"

Laney turned her head as did Cowboy when a leggy redhead strode across the room, latching onto his coiled muscular arm. His nose crinkled. Then a practiced lazy smile flitted across his handsome features. Those baby blue lagoon eyes of his dropped to half-mast. A whirring of the air around Laney fluffed her shoulder-length hair as another figure rushed forward.

The willowy blond from Information seized Cowboy Kai by his other arm. He inclined his head as the I-Can't-Be-Bothered airport employee whispered something for his ears only. Too far away for their conversation to register—and who cared?—she did catch Cowboy's deep-throated chuckle in response to whatever witticism Blondie had murmured.

Typical. She'd seen his macho, arrogant type many times following her father around the globe in the rolling stone life of Uncle Sam's army. Laney folded her hands in her lap. His kind loved the fluffy kittens of the world like Blondie and the redhead. He probably wasn't a real cowboy, either. Probably didn't know one end of a horse from a—

A mountainous shadow inserted itself between Laney and the fluorescent lighting of the terminal. She jerked at the sight of Cowboy looming over her.

"Ms. Carrigan, I presume?" A mocking smile flickered at the corners of his lips.

Laney's hackles rose, and she hunched her shoulders as she struggled to rise from her awkward position on the floor. The heel of her shoe caught on the handle of her bag and she fell— make that *sprawled*—into his arms.

Wishing she could sink into the floor, she felt the blush matching and mounting from beneath the collar of her pink shirtwaist blouse.

Great, elegant as always.

But she'd give him full kudos for quick reflexes.

In a full face-plant against the blue fabric of his shirt, Laney noted—in the half-second before Cowboy pulled his own nose out of her hair—an enticing blend of smells on the man, a spicy aftershave like her father wore, cocoa butter, and something indefinable that belonged to him alone. Awkward . . . this was long past getting out of hand.

Laney took herself in hand and cleared her throat.

Cowboy, his hands wrapped around her upper arms, set her aright upon her two left feet. His black-fringed eyes— eyelashes the envy of any girl—blinked. Not that there was anything remotely girlish about him.

His fingers lingered. Stepping back, Laney almost fell again over her suitcase. His hand shot out, restoring her balance. He nudged her bag out of the way with the pointed toe of his boot.

Was it her imagination or did a rosy flush darken his sculpted cheekbones? "Carrigan, right?"

She shook free of his grip. "And you would know that how?" Settling her hands on her hips, she looked past him to where the two fluffy kittens glared mayhem in her direction. "Who are you?"

He jammed his hands into the front pockets of his pants. "Kai Barnes. I'm here to perform an SAR for Auntie Teah. A search—"

"I know what an SAR is, Mr. Barnes. Search and rescue."

The full beam of his oceanic orbs lasered her. She extended her neck upward, refusing to let his six-foot height intimidate her.

"Sure." A derisive smirk crossed his too-handsome-to-live features. "I forgot about your military background."

"I take it you're military, too?" Should've seen it sooner, but the boots had thrown her off. She could spot 'em, all right. That distinct swagger, that I'm licensed to kill attitude, that . . .

"Army pilot." His eyes shuttered again. "Former. Flew SAR in medevacs." He removed his hands from his pockets and crossed his arms over his chest. His mouth flatlined. "Search and rescue seems to be what I do best." His gaze raked her over. "I'll take you to Teah, who's waiting for us at the ranch. My—"

"I'm not going anywhere with you." Laney's chest puffed out. "I was told to wait for my Aunt Teah or Elyse. I don't know you from Adam. You could be some psycho cowboy serial killer for all I know." She crossed her arms, mirroring his stance.

Kai raised his eyes toward the ceiling, his jaw working. An exasperated sigh rose from the depths of his being, rolling through the airwaves like a rumbling volcanic eruption. "Teah's not your real aunt." He stabbed Laney with a fierce look. "If you are who you claim to be . . ."

Laney fixed him with a matching glare.

245

"She and your mother were first cousins, which makes Elyse, Teah's daughter, a more distant cousin. Auntie is a term of respect for elders in our Hawai'ian culture."

"Hawai'ian? Our?" She let her eyes roam up and down his muscular form in a deliberate repetition of his scathing perusal of her earlier. Kai flushed again. This time though—and she could tell the difference—with anger.

Muttering something under his breath, with a sudden move, Kai whipped a brown leather wallet from one of the ubiquitous pockets lining his pants. He extracted a driver's license and held it to her face. "Kai Barnes. My address—Franklin Ranch. Near Waimea. There's been a slight emergency with Tutu Mily, so they sent—"

"Tutu? Mily?" Laney's arms dropped to her sides. "Do you mean Miliana Franklin, my grandmother? What's happened?"

"Your understanding of our culture underwhelms me. Tutu means grandmother. And yes, I refer to Miliana Kanakele Franklin, although whether she's actually your grandmother or not remains to be seen."

Laney stiffened.

"Teah said she'd explain when we reached the ranch. Until then, if you want to meet your Hawai'ian relatives, then I suggest . . ." His arm swept the room and pointed at the glass doors.

"Fine. Have it your way." Laney bent to retrieve her bag but found Kai to be quicker, his hand grasping the handle. She tugged.

He held on.

Laney let go.

So, he was a gentleman, too.

"This puny thing it?" He heaved it to his shoulder.

"I learned a long time ago to travel light."

Laney sashayed past him toward the double doors and the parking lot, pretending as always she knew exactly where she was headed. And if things got too uncomfortable with these virtual strangers . . . She fingered her escape hatch in the pocket of her skirt, her return ticket via Jakarta.

She'd give them three weeks. Three weeks before she winged out to her next assignment. She eyeballed her teeth-clenched companion.

Maybe sooner. They didn't know it yet, but the moment Cowboy showed up, her clock started ticking.

A disconcerted feeling settled over her at the truth of that statement.

Ticking in more ways than one.

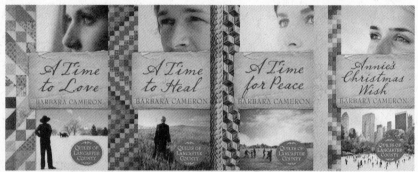

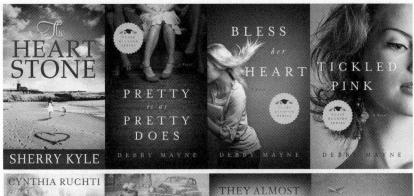
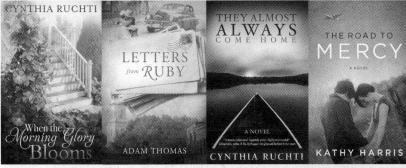
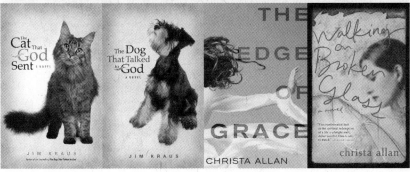